The Circle

By RW Biga

Copyright ©2023 by RW Biga

All right reserved. No part of this book can be reproduced in any form without the written consent of the author: including photocopy, recording, or any storage information and retrieval system, without the written permission of the copyright owner. This book is fiction. Any resemblance to people or places is purely coincidental.

Acknowledgements

I'd like to thank the following people for the support on this book: Kasia Wasilewska, Tim Kessel, Amy Scott, Rebecca Klassen, Deanna Kuempel, Kerry Piazza, Panagiota Weddel, Caeli Sieverts, Kevin Lewis, Barbara Paine, Suzanne Augusta, and the Starvin Artist company for my book cover.

RW Biga's other works.

Fate's Collision
https://www.amazon.com/Fates-Collision-RW-Biga-ebook/dp/B09NQP5CKW/

The Education of Adam
https://www.amazon.com/Education-Adam-R-W-Biga-ebook/dp/B08P2C7RZK/

Snowbound
https://www.amazon.com/Snowbound-RW-Biga-ebook/dp/B0BLJ27KW5/

The Call

Kyle didn't recognize the number on his caller ID. The number 555-847-7269 had the area code of his youth, making him wonder who could be calling him. It was not yet 10 am, so it was probably not a telemarketer. It had been a few years since anyone from back home had given him a ring. A foreboding sense stopped him from reaching for the receiver. After five rings, the user hung up. Kyle tapped his fingers on the desk in his home office, waiting to see if they left a voicemail, but they didn't. In the past, he had received various phone calls with unrecognized numbers from people who left strange voicemails, so he felt nervous whenever that occurred.

After a few more minutes, the phone rang again. It was the same number. Taking a deep breath, he picked up the receiver.

"Hello?" Kyle answered.

"Hello, is this Kyle Brighton?"

"Yes, it is. Who am I speaking with?"

"My name is Genevieve Fremont."

That last name reminded him of his old friend, Dave Fremont. Dave and Kyle had lived in the town of Woodbrook, Illinois, when they were in grade and high school. They had been friends for years but had stopped talking over a decade ago. Dave's mother wasn't Genevieve, so Kyle was curious as to who this woman on the phone was.

"Hello, are you related to Dave?"

There was a slight pause on the other end of the phone.

"I'm his cousin," she said. "I was told by Dave to call you."

"Is there something going on here?"

There was another pause. Kyle thought about the last time he had seen Dave. It was a month after they'd graduated high school. They'd seen each other at the local movie theatre but had been with different groups of friends. They acknowledged each other, but that was it. Kyle felt like they'd drifted apart towards the end of their senior year, and that cold meeting had solidified it. A few weeks after they'd seen each other at the theatre, they both went away to different colleges and never attempted to contact each other again.

"He wanted me to tell you..." Genevieve stopped, choking up.

Kyle waited for a response, but nothing came.

"Please tell me what you were about to say. I know it might be difficult, but I need to know."

"Dave is gone. He passed over a week ago. He requested that I call you after he'd gone. He was insistent."

Kyle couldn't say anything at that moment. He was at a loss for words. Genevieve sobbed gently, and he didn't know what to say to make her stop.

"He wanted me to contact you," she continued, "and have you contact the four others in your group to come back to Woodbrook."

"What four others?" he asked.

She paused, then said, "The circle is broken."

Kyle knew what that meant. He hadn't heard that phrase for at least a dozen years. It was something that he had hoped not to hear for decades to come.

"I understand," Kyle said. "I know what I must do now. Thank you for calling me."

"I don't know what the circle is," Genevieve said. "Dave left a note a few weeks before he died and instructed me not to ask about it."

"What happened to him?" Kyle asked.

"He had cancer. He kept it quiet up until the last few weeks. He requested to be cremated and for there not to be a funeral. His ashes are at his house; the one he grew up in."

Kyle knew the four people he needed to contact: Erica Fernandez, Alex Overhill, Owen Seward, and Lauren Stratton. It had been at least six years since he had seen any of them in person. He'd bumped into Alex in Chicago at a Cubs game. They'd acknowledged each other and went their separate ways.

"I know what I need to do," Kyle said. "I don't have all their numbers, but I'll figure it out. I'm sure some of them kept in contact with each other."

"Whose numbers do you have?" Genevieve asked.

Kyle looked at his phone and saw that he had two of them. "I have numbers for Alex and Erica. I'll call them individually and see if they have numbers for the other two."

"Thank you, Kyle. I wish I knew what this was about, but Dave mentioned that he wanted to keep this secret."

If that was what Dave wanted, then Kyle decided he would also stay quiet about it.

"Will you be around Woodbrook when I get there?" Kyle asked.

"No," she replied. "I don't have any relatives left there. His parents have both passed. I'm in Raleigh, North Carolina now."

"I'm sorry to hear about his parents. They were both nice to me."

"I believe that we met once, Kyle."

Kyle didn't remember anyone with her name but pretended that he did to avoid any awkwardness. "Your name sounds familiar."

"It was at his high school graduation party. I believe you were hanging around with Erica. Dave used to call me "Gena-weird.""

Kyle and Erica had been at Dave's graduation party. He didn't remember much about it except that Dave's rich uncle had given Dave a five-thousand-dollar check. Dave wasn't shy about showing it to all his friends. Kyle had felt jealous.

"Now I remember," Kyle said, even though he didn't.

"Anyways, that was a long time ago," Genevieve said. "It was nice talking to you, Kyle. I hope you're able to accomplish whatever Dave wanted your group to do. He was very cryptic about what he wanted."

Kyle felt that Genevieve's tone was probing, but there was no way he'd tell her about the circle if Dave hadn't wanted him to.

"Nice talk to you, too."

"One more thing," Genevieve said.

"Okay."

"Like I mentioned, his ashes are in his house. They're on top of the fireplace in an urn. He said that you and your friends would know what to do with them. I was also told to leave the house key in the flowerpot on the porch. I left it there today, so please go there and get it soon."

"Thank you," Kyle said. "If I can get together with the others, I'm sure we'll be able to do what we promised somehow."

"The ownership of the house will be given over to another person in ten days. I don't know who or how it will be handed over. I only know it's not me, and I'm ok with that. I'm actually a bit relieved, as I have my own issues going on right now, and I don't have time to sort out a house sale in Illinois. He must have planned this out a while back, as that amount of time seems quick to get the house affairs settled. You can use Dave's house to your liking until then; Dave mentioned you and the others could."

"Goodbye and thank you, Kyle."

"Thank you for doing what he requested."

Kyle put the phone down and put his head on the desk. He couldn't believe that his childhood friend was gone. Even though they hadn't spoken for years, it didn't feel that long. The same went for the other four old friends he needed to contact. The four of them had all been together a few times as kids; there was a childhood of memories. He knew that going back to his hometown would bring back many more memories. Despite being in his mid-thirties, Kyle remembered their times together vividly.

The call occurred at the right time. He was currently on the third day of his two-week vacation from work. He'd planned to drive to New Buffalo, Michigan, and stay at a hotel in the area for a few days. That was two days away, so he quickly called the hotel and canceled his reservation.

Since Kyle refused to use social media, he hadn't kept up with anyone from Woodbrook. Some of his coworkers teased him about not using social platforms, but he wanted to keep his life private. He hoped that Erica or Alex had contact details for Owen and Lauren.

He decided that contacting Erica first was his best chance. It had to be at least three years since he'd heard her voice, and about eight years since he had seen her in person. Before that last call, they had emailed or called each other at least once a year. He'd last got a call from her in the middle of the day, asking how he was doing. It was a short call, as she'd suddenly had to go. She promised to call him back but never did. It seemed like there might've been someone in the background of where she was as she kept putting him on hold. Kyle thought about calling her back but was reluctant as the call had seemed strange. His guess was that she didn't want someone near her to know she was talking to him. He figured she'd called him impulsively and didn't know what to say.

If Erica didn't answer the phone, Kyle would call Alex. When he'd seen him at the Cubs game, they hadn't spoken. Kyle had given him a nod from across the crowd and then disappeared down the stadium stairs. Alex hadn't nodded back or attempted to come over.

With Owen, it had been about twelve years since they'd seen each other. They'd met at a local bar after Kyle graduated from Northwestern, because Owen was moving away to Minnesota a few weeks later. Owen hadn't gone to college and worked as a realtor like his father. They didn't talk about much except about how Owen was making a killing in his job. Owen had talked about it so much that Kyle got annoyed. Kyle did try to call him one time a few years later, but it was no longer Owen's number.

Lauren had gone to college at some small place in Indiana that Kyle couldn't remember. Kyle had liked her as a teen and sometimes thought of her when he saw an attractive blonde. She never reached out to Kyle once she'd moved away. Kyle wanted to call her but always felt too afraid to do so. He feared she would think he was strange for calling her out of the blue.

About five years ago, Erica called Kyle and mentioned that she and Lauren had lost touch too. Lauren's family had moved out of the neighborhood within a year of her going away to college. Kyle had the feeling that Lauren had wanted to get away from Woodbrook. It might have been because Lauren didn't enjoy her home life because her mother was so strict.

"The circle is broken," he said to himself.

He never thought that he'd hear that phrase ever again. It had meant something to them as children when they'd made the pact. Now they had to fulfill that pact as adults.

Erica

Kyle looked up Erica's number again and paused before dialing, thinking about how to approach the call. He didn't want to blurt out 'the circle is broken' right away, but he also wanted to get to the point. After a few minutes of thought, he decided to just call her and take it from there.

The phone rang, but no one picked up. Kyle didn't want to leave a voicemail, so he hung up. He thought about texting her, but that seemed too informal and improper for sharing the sad news about Dave. Hearing her voice would be more pleasant too.

He tried her again, and a few minutes later, she picked up the phone.

"Hello?" Erica said suspiciously.

"Hi Erica, it's Kyle Brighton from Woodbrook."

"Well, hello, Kyle. How are you doing?"

Kyle decided that he should just say it. "The circle is broken."

"I remember that saying. What's happened?"

"Unfortunately," Kyle said, "Dave Fremont has passed away. His cousin just called and said we need to go back to his parents' house. Dave was cremated, and his ashes are there in an urn."

On the other end of the phone, Kyle could hear Erica sniffle. He didn't know what to say, so he waited.

"That's so unfortunate," Erica said after sniffling again. "I thought about calling him just last week. It has been years since I've seen or talked to him. I wish that I'd called him when I thought about it."

"His cousin told me that he had cancer. I think that he wanted to be alone. Don't feel bad about it. I don't know what he was doing with his life. I'd like to get some answers. I'm going back to Woodbrook."

"I'll go back with you. We all made a promise, and we should fulfill it, Kyle."

"Agreed."

"When are you going back there?" she asked.

"I'm going to try to get a flight to Illinois tonight. If not, I'll drive there. That'd be a six to seven-hour drive, though."

"Where are you living nowadays, Kyle?"

"I'm just outside of Cincinnati. How about you?"

"Orlando, Florida. I'm glad I didn't change my number after I moved here from Atlanta."

"I've never been to Atlanta, but I've been to Orlando," Kyle said.

"I moved here for a new job. I've only been here six months, and I like it much better than Atlanta."

"I'll look for a flight. I should be there by tomorrow."

"Excuse me for a minute, Kyle."

It sounded like she had put her phone down on a surface. Kyle could hear something in the background. As he listened attentively, he thought it might be her closet door being opened and closed. A minute went by until he heard her pick up the cellphone again.

"Sorry, Kyle. I just had to see if I still had my yearbook. I wanted to look at our graduation year and take a look at Dave's face. I found it in my closet. I haven't thought of him in a while. I needed a reminder of his face."

"No problem. I don't even know if I have mine anymore. Thinking about it now, I hope I do have it somewhere."

"I'll bring it with me. Maybe all of us can look at it."

"Sounds good, Erica."

"On another note," she said.

"Yes?"

"Have you told the others?"

"I haven't. I have Alex's number, but I don't have Owen's or Lauren's. Do you happen to have them?"

"Let me look," Erica said. Kyle waited.

A few seconds later, she said, "I have both their numbers. Do you want me to call them, Kyle?"

"No," Kyle replied. "It was part of our pact that the first one contacted would contact the others. I want to keep this as we promised."

"That's right!" Erica said. "We did say that. I'm glad you remembered. I'll never forget our promise, but I forgot that part."

"It's okay."

"I wonder what else I may have forgotten," Erica said.

"I remember everything. It has stayed with me this whole time. I'm good at things like that. I think that's why Dave wanted his cousin to contact me first. Can you text me Owen's and Lauren's numbers? I'll call Alex next."

"Sure," Erica said. "No problem. I'm going to start packing. I'll see if I can get the earliest flight tomorrow. I'll text you when I'm back in Chicago."

"Thank you. I can't wait."

"Will you go to a hotel or stay at Dave's house?"

"His cousin is letting me stay there. There should be plenty of rooms for all of us."

"I didn't think about that. I can stay in one of the rooms if you don't mind, Kyle."

"Then we're set. See you soon, Erica."

After saying goodbye, Kyle hung up the phone and looked for flights from Cincinnati to Chicago. He picked the one that left around 3:45 pm. It was about an hour and a half, so he'd arrive at

4:17 pm due to the time zone change. It had been a long time since Kyle had been on a flight, so he bought a first-class ticket.

After booking the flight, a text came in from Erica. It had both Owen's and Lauren's numbers. Kyle didn't recognize the area codes. As with Erica, he figured that they'd moved out of state too. Many people from Woodbrook had done the same thing. Before calling the two of them, he wanted to call Alex first. He had a feeling, as always, that he might be the most troublesome. Hopefully, Kyle was wrong about that.

Alex

Kyle thought about how to tell Alex the bad news, unsure how to do it. Alex had usually been in a joking mood when they'd hung out, so Kyle wasn't sure if he was going to take him seriously. In high school, Alex didn't get good grades, and was often sent to the principal's office for interrupting class. Despite graduating, he was in the lower ten percent of the class rankings. Kyle thought Alex was much smarter than he acted, but it never showed in high school. Alex had always had a knack for fixing things such as cars and making repairs around the house. One time, Alex fixed a broken ceiling fan's electrical output. This was when Alex was seventeen years of age, and to Kyle's knowledge, it was without any training.

    Kyle dialed Alex's number. He let it ring ten times before he hung up. There'd been no voicemail option, so there was no way to leave a message. He thought about texting, but he felt that wouldn't be as effective as saying those four important words.

    As Kyle was about to call again, Alex called him back.

    "Hello, who's this?"

    "Hi Alex, this is Kyle Brighton. Do you remember me?"

    "Of course I do, shithead. How are you doing?"

Before he could consider answering Alex's question, he found himself blurting, "The circle is broken, Alex."

Alex paused. "I remember that phrase. I never thought I'd hear it again. In fact, I hoped I never would."

"It's Dave Fremont. He passed away about a week ago. His cousin Genevieve called me earlier today to tell me, and she mentioned those four words. She doesn't know what those words mean, though."

"What happened to him?" Alex asked.

"Cancer."

"That sucks, Kyle."

"Yes, it does."

"On another note, I'm glad he didn't tell her what it all means," Alex said. "She was a bitch. She always thought that I liked her. I never did. She was nasty. Since I used to joke around a lot when we were teenagers, she thought I was joking when I denied liking her."

"I remember that you used to joke around a lot," Kyle said.

Alex cleared his throat. "I'm not like that anymore, at least not as much. I got in trouble in college, and I learned my lesson from that. At least, I think I did."

Kyle couldn't imagine Alex being serious. For as long as he'd known him, there had always been a goofy side to him. If that part of his personality was gone, Kyle would feel like he'd be meeting an entirely new person.

"Well, maybe it was for the best, Alex."

"Maybe some other time I can tell you about, Kyle."

"Dave wanted the five of us to get back together. I already talked to Erica, and she's going back to Woodbrook as soon as she can. I'm going to leave today after I get in contact with Owen and Lauren. Will you be able to meet us within the next day or so?"

"Well…"

Kyle could feel an excuse coming. Alex had always been flaky, but to blow the group off at this time would be a downright low thing to do. Kyle wasn't going to take 'no' for an answer.

"Well, what?" Kyle asked.

"I sort of don't have a way to get there. I'm in between jobs right now and don't have a lot of money. My divorce didn't help things. Luckily, we didn't have any kids."

Kyle wondered if Alex was going to ask him for money. When they were teenagers, Alex would often ask people for money and never pay them back. Kyle hoped he wasn't still like that.

"Are you still working as a carpenter, Alex?"

"I do when I get the opportunity. Some people think that I price myself out, but I don't think so. I know I do good work, so I want to get paid for it. If that means that I don't work sometimes, so be it. I deserve to be paid well, and I won't let anyone use me."

"So you work freelance?" Kyle asked.

Alex was silent for a few seconds, then replied, "My dad taught me a lot. You remember me fixing a few things in your room? He also taught me about people. He often rejected jobs when he thought that someone wanted to lowball him. I've kept that same attitude, and no one will change that."

Alex sounded like he thought the world owed him something. Kyle didn't like it when people were like that. If it weren't for Dave's wishes, Kyle would've said goodbye and ended their conversation.

"That's your choice," Kyle said. "You know what's best for you. It's your life."

He wondered if Alex might hang up on him. His tone gave Kyle the impression that he was about to get irritated. Kyle would call him back if he hung up. Dave's wishes was the most important thing right now.

"Yes, it's my choice, Kyle."

To change the subject, Kyle said the first thing that came into his head. "Do you still like to collect baseball cards?"

"I do. Not just baseball cards. I collect electronics too. All kinds of gadgets. I won big on a football bet once and bought an arcade machine, Mortal Kombat, like that one at the arcade in Woodbrook."

Kyle could see why Alex didn't have much money. He'd never learned how to budget, gambling and blowing his money on things he could live without.

"I stopped a while ago on the cards," Kyle said. "I'm not much of a collector these days. I just invest a little bit in stocks."

"Never been my forte, Kyle. I guess I'm more reckless. My ex-wife seems to think so. I heard that from her a few times."

"Speaking of baseball, the Cubs did well last year, Alex." Hopefully 2016 is their year."

"Let's hope, Kyle. Maybe I can put some money on them. Maybe a grand or so. I don't have much now, though."

Kyle knew he had to find a way for Alex to get back to their hometown. He wasn't even sure if Alex had enough money to make it to Woodbrook.

"Where are you living now?" Kyle asked.

"I'm in Milwaukee. I didn't move too far away. I've thought about going back to Woodbrook, but I haven't had a good enough excuse."

Milwaukee was only about seventy-five miles from Woodbrook. He could easily take a train or bus. Kyle wouldn't mind paying for that, as it wouldn't be too much money.

"How about I pay for a ticket for you to come back to Dave's old house? I believe there's a train that stops about five miles away on the edge of town. I remember there being one when we all used to live back home. If it doesn't stop there anymore, I can pay for a bus. Will that work for you?"

"Why'd you want to do that, Kyle?"

"Because we all made a promise to each other. Dave made a request, so I think we all owe it to him, especially now he's passed away."

"You're right, Kyle. We did make a promise. I haven't been the most reliable person with promises in my life. However, I should fulfill this one."

"That's a good choice," Kyle said. "I hope everyone can."

"I may not be able to pay you back for a bit, Kyle. I'm down to my last few dollars due to the recession that's going on."

Kyle knew there wasn't a recession. He'd studied economics in college and knew there hadn't been one in at least eighteen months. To avoid an argument, Kyle decided to not correct him. He might ask him about it later, but not now.

"It's ok," Kyle said. "Consider it a gift. I'll be staying at Dave's house for a few days, so you can stay with me if you want. Some of the others might stay here too. Erica is going to for sure. I just spoke with her."

"Sounds good," Alex said.

Kyle waited to see if there was any negative reaction to the mention of Erica, but there was not. As teens, there was some tension between Alex and Erica. It was petty stuff, but Alex might still have that those memories in his mind.

"You're still in Woodbrook, Kyle?"

"No, I'm in Cincinnati. I plan to be at Dave's by tonight, though. His cousin left me a key, so I'll stay there until I feel it's time to leave."

"Okay, see if you can find me a train or bus. I can try to pay you back when I get money."

Kyle stayed on the line and looked for buses and trains on his laptop that stopped near Woodbrook. After searching for a few minutes, he found a train that arrived at 7:54 p.m. near Woodbrook.

"There's a train that gets in at 7:54 tonight. I'll order the ticket now and email it to you. My flight gets in at 4:17 today at O'Hare, so I'll have enough time to meet you at the station. If my flight is delayed for some reason, I'll text you. I doubt it will be, though."

Alex gave Kyle his email address. "Thank you for doing this, Kyle."

"No problem."

"It's been a long time since we last met. I think I last saw you at a Cubs game years back. It'll be great to see everyone. That's if they all decide to meet up with us again."

"I've got a feeling that we'll all get back together," Kyle said, not wanting to mention the Cubs game. That day had felt awkward enough. "Once we settle everything on Dave's behalf, we should all go out."

"That's a good idea. I haven't been out in a bit. Milwaukee hasn't been very fun for me."

"Call me when your train is near the station."

"See you then, Kyle. Bye."

Kyle said goodbye and hung up. He was glad he'd found a way for Alex to return to Woodbrook. Despite Alex's lack of funds, he hadn't needed any persuasion. Now it was time to see if Owen and Lauren needed persuading.

Owen

Kyle wanted to make the call to Owen short and sweet, as he had to prepare for his flight. If Owen didn't answer on the first try, Kyle would start packing and try again later.

"Hello?" Owen said, picking up on the first ring.

"Hi Owen. This is Kyle Brighton. I got your number from Erica Fernandez."

'Hi Kyle, it has been quite a few years. How's it going?"

Kyle decided to take the same approach he had with Alex and get straight to the point. "The circle is broken."

"Can you say that again?" Owen asked in disbelief.

"The circle is broken. I was told to contact you about it."

"I remember that phrase well, Kyle."

"Dave Fremont has passed away. It was cancer. His cousin Genevieve contacted me, and I just got off the phone with Erica and Alex. They're coming back to Woodbrook. I still need to contact is Lauren."

"I wish that you'd called me for another reason, Kyle. I'll miss him."

"Same here, Owen."

"As for Lauren, I used to speak to her a lot, Kyle. She's maybe thirty minutes from where I live. She was divorced a few years back."

"Did you ever get married, Owen?"

"Nope," Owen replied. "I've no interest in doing so. I thought I did and was actually about to get engaged, but backed out."

"Alex has also been divorced. Not sure what happened there." Kyle said.

Owen let out a quick laugh. "I'm not surprised about him. I've heard that he has become quite unreliable. He always needs money."

Kyle didn't want to say anything bad about Alex to Owen.

"Well, Alex is coming back to meet us at Dave's house. Will you be able to make it?"

"Sure," Owen replied. "I can take a flight and get there as soon as I can."

"Perfect," Kyle said.

"I'll call Lauren and see if she wants to travel with me."

"Wait on that. I'll call Lauren to tell her about Dave," Kyle said. "I called Erica and Alex already, so I might as well call her too."

"You do that," Owen said.

"Just have her call me after you call her, Kyle."

"Where do both of you live nowadays?"

"We're both near Franklin, Tennessee. I'm in the city itself and she is in a smaller suburb. She's maybe fifteen miles from me. I didn't even know she lived here until she contacted me via Facebook. I moved from Minnesota a few years back. It's much better here in Tennessee. I looked for your profile a few months back and couldn't find one for you."

Since Kyle sometimes worked in criminal law, he wanted to stay anonymous. Even if he hadn't been in that type of law, he would've stayed off social media. He liked privacy, peace, and quiet. His firm had a website, and his name was it; he felt that was enough.

"I stay away from putting my private life online. I think it's better that way," Kyle said.

"That's understandable."

"There should be plenty of flights out of Nashville so that's good," Kyle said to change the subject.

"You're right. I often travel for business, so I know that airport well," Owen said. "What's your business, Owen?"

"I own a house-building company. I felt it was a natural progression after being a realtor.
The market in Tennessee has exploded. So many people are moving here. It makes me some good dough. Of course, my ability to soak up so much business knowledge helped."

Kyle had thought about moving to Tennessee at one time. He liked the no income tax aspect of the state. He'd never got the nerve to do it, though. His job was safe at the law firm, and he didn't want to go freelance.

"It'll be nice to see all of you again," Kyle said. "It has been way too long."

"Agreed, Kyle."

"Once we've done what we promised, then what?" Owen asked.

"I've no idea. Dave's house will be handed over to someone else in about ten days, so I guess I'll go back to Cincinnati then."

"You live in that dump of a city?" Owen asked.

"Just outside of it. I'm in a nice suburb."

Kyle didn't think Cincinnati was a bad place. There were some bad parts like everywhere else, but he felt it had a bad reputation, mostly among those who'd never visited. He felt certain that Owen had never been there based on his comment. Kyle sometimes went into the city to visit the Zoo and Botanical Gardens, and watch the Reds play baseball.

"I'm going to look for flights now, Kyle. I can stay a few days, but I'll have to get back for work. We have a huge project that's starting soon."

"Sounds good, Owen. I'm not even sure what our old neighborhood looks like anymore. Maybe a nostalgia tour will be in order."

"That sounds like a plan. I might also need to book a hotel in the area."

"You can always stay at Dave's house with Alex and me. He can't afford to stay at a hotel. Erica will be staying there too."

"Yeah, like I said before, Alex is the guy always needs money."

"Try to not mention money to Alex, Owen. I think it's a touchy subject for him."

"Okay, "Owen replied. "I'll try to stay off that subject.

"As for Erica," Owen said, "I wonder if she's still hot. I saw her on Instagram, and she was nice."

"I'm not sure," Kyle said as he wondered if Owen would make a move on Erica when they met up. He hoped not, as Owen would probably be enough to irritate her.

"For whatever reason, she either unfriended me or canceled her account," said Owen. "I guess I'll be able to find out this weekend."

"Possibly," Kyle said, "I'm sure she just had enough of putting her life out there for everyone to see."

Kyle didn't want to talk with Owen anymore. He was getting a vibe that Owen would be a pain to be around for the next few days. His cockiness was already irritating. Kyle was usually a good judge of character, but he hoped he was wrong.

"I must go now, Owen. I need to start packing and catch my flight. I'm picking up Alex at the train station shortly after my flight gets in."

"I'll look for flights now. I think I might stay at a hotel for at least the first night and take it from there, Kyle. Maybe I'll change my mind on that, though."

"Sounds good," Kyle said. "Text me once your flight lands."

"Will do, Kyle. Talk to you later."

After Kyle hung up, he wondered why Owen wanted to stay at a hotel and not Dave's house. Did Owen have an issue with one of the other three? It could be due to Erica unfriending him, or maybe even Alex, as money was something Owen liked to dwell on. Why had Erica unfriended him? If there was an issue, Kyle hoped that it wouldn't ruin their time together.

Lauren

All that was left was to call Lauren. Kyle was glad that everyone else was able to come so far. Before calling her, he thought about looking at his high school yearbook to see what everyone looked like back then. It had been at least ten years since he had looked, so it was a good refresher. After spending five minutes looking for the yearbook, he found it.

He looked at his own picture quickly and then found Lauren's. It made his heart jump. He had a crush on her as a teen, but nothing ever came of it. He never got to know her as much as he wanted to. During their junior and senior years of high school, he kept thinking of ways to get to know her better. Unfortunately, the time ran out, and they both went their separate ways after high school.

When he called Lauren, she picked up after one ring.

"Hello Kyle," Lauren said.

"Hi Lauren, how did you know it was me?"

"Owen texted me and said you would be calling. He didn't tell me why, though."

Kyle thought about how he'd asked Owen to not call her. Owen got around that by texting instead. That irritated Kyle enough that he decided not to tell Lauren about Owen wanting to travel with her to Woodbrook.

"Okay, good," Kyle said. "I wanted you to hear it from me."

"What is it?"

"The circle is broken, Lauren."

Lauren gasped. "Was it Alex, Erica, or Dave?"

"It was Dave. He passed away a week ago. His cousin contacted me and asked me to return to his parent's house."

"And he wanted all of us to return, right?" Lauren asked in a choked-up tone.

"Yes, that's correct."

There was a slight pause of a few seconds in which she said nothing.

"Now?" she asked after sniffling.

"As soon as possible. Owen, Alex, and Erica can all come by tomorrow. I'll be there tonight. Can you join us?"

"Well," she said. "I have my son Taylor until tomorrow. I'll make sure I get there like we all promised to."

"Okay, so maybe get there in two days?" Kyle asked.

A chomping sound occurred on the other end of the phone. "I can see if I can make it there tomorrow or the next day at the latest. My ex may be able to take Taylor tonight. I'll ask him once I get off the phone."

"If you could get there by then, that'd be great," Kyle said.

"We all made a promise, Kyle. I'm one to keep such things. The Fremont Treehouse Club will always live on."

Kyle hadn't heard that name in many years. He smiled to himself. It was the name of their club, just him, Erica, Lauren, Owen, Alex, and Dave. They often referred to it as the FTC. They formed it one night a long time ago and used Dave's last name in the title. All six of them were present in Dave's treehouse when they agreed on the name.

"I haven't seen you since high school, Lauren. It's been too long."

"Yes...it has. My life is so different now that I have Taylor and live alone."

"How old is Taylor?"

There was more chomping. "He's going to be four soon. He's the only thing good that came out of my marriage."

"I'm sorry to hear about your divorce. Alex was married, too but, got divorced. Not sure what happened there."

"I'm not surprised. He called me a few years ago, asking for money. When I said no, he stopped calling me. I was kind of relieved, to be honest."

"It sounds like he has a reputation for not being reliable, Lauren."

"Sorry, but I'm eating some carrots right now. I'm on a mostly vegetarian diet, and I want to stick to it."

"Good for you," Kyle said with sincerity. "It's always good to stick to goals."

"I needed to make a change in my life. I thought I'd met my next husband, but he turned out to be a dud. He reminds me of Alex; he became unreliable. I'm glad I saw that before he proposed. I can tell you more about him once I get back to Woodbrook.

"Sounds good, Lauren."

"Did you ever get married, Kyle?"

"I didn't. I've had some girlfriends but none that ended up being anything."

"Is anyone else in our group married?"

"Not that I know of," Kyle replied. "We're all still relatively young so that could change."

"Let's hope. I haven't had the best of luck with men."

Kyle was usually too busy with work to find someone he could consistently see. He had gone on some dates. Unfortunately, he didn't seem to click with anyone. Most of his friends where he lived were married, but it never really felt important to him.

"I guess that I haven't found the right one," he said. "I'm a lawyer, so I'm often busy. Luckily, I'm not in the middle of a case so I can take off for the next few days. Most of the people I know are married, though."

"Are you saving the world with your lawyering?" Lauren asked.

"I don't really enjoy it much anymore. I won a big case last year, but after that, I found I don't have the same motivation. Not sure if it will come back any time soon."

"I wanted to be a lawyer a few years ago. That all changed when I had my son. Now I work at the local library. I got my bachelor's in biology and never did anything with it. My ex had some money, so I didn't have the push I needed. I regret not pursuing a master's or more."

"There's still time," Kyle said.

"You're right, Kyle."

"It was good talking to you. I need to get ready so I can get to the airport. I'm picking Alex up at the train station right after I land."

"I hope he makes it, Kyle. He gives me a bad vibe. Maybe he's changed since the last time I spoke with him."

All the negativity surrounding Alex was starting to bother Kyle. Kyle wondered if Alex knew how they felt about him.

"We'll see, Lauren. I bought him a train ticket, so hopefully he'll make it. If he doesn't, then I don't know what to say."

"Anyways," Lauren said, "I'll be friendly towards him. I don't know his whole situation."

"Good idea. I know Alex wants to come to Woodbrook and keep the same promise we all made. Please send me a text when you know you'll be there. If it takes two days, that's fine, Lauren. I don't want you to rush if you have other responsibilities."

"My guess is that I'll leave tomorrow and be there by nighttime. Everyone else should be there by then, right?"

Kyle hesitated. "If all goes to plan. If it takes a bit longer, I'll understand. This was all on short notice."

"You were always understanding. I wish that I could've said the same about my ex-husband."

Lauren mentioning her ex a lot made Kyle wonder if she was still in love with him. There might have been more to their divorce than he realized. He now wanted to know what made her marry him in the first place. When Lauren was a teenager, she seemed to possess the most sense out of all of them. Once, she'd refused to get into a car after a party where they were drunk. Because of her stubbornness, they wound up walking home.

"Thank you. Owen might want to fly with you. He mentioned you lived near him."

There was silence for a moment. "That's alright. I'll go by myself."

"I'll be waiting for your text. Talk to you again soon," Kyle said.

"Yes, I look forward to seeing all of you. Bye, Kyle."

Kyle hung up. He felt his short conversation with Lauren was the best he'd had of all four. Her voice was pleasant, and it made him think of the crush he'd had on her when they were teens. He'd never told her, and nothing had ever happened between them. In the years since he had seen her, he wondered what it would've been like if they'd dated.

Now that all of them had been contacted and confirmed they were coming, Kyle felt relieved. The promise that all of them made would be fulfilled. After his flight and car rental were set, it was time to go.

Getting Ready

Kyle got ready for his flight in a short amount of time. There wasn't much to prepare that would need to be tended to while he was away. He didn't have any pets, and his bills were paid electronically.

For his trip, he just took a carry-on spinner. The cab to pick him up arrived a half hour later.

Once he got to the airport, he decided to text Alex.

KYLE: Hey Alex, are you on your train yet?

After twenty minutes, Alex hadn't replied. Kyle wanted to send another text but decided against it. If he sent too many texts, Alex might get irritated and not respond. Instead, he texted Owen.

KYLE: Hey, are you and Lauren going on the same flight?
OWEN: No, we're not. She's coming in tomorrow but not sure what time. I might be delayed a bit. I'll probably be there tomorrow night.
KYLE: Sounds good

OWEN: Not sure why she doesn't want to go with me

KYLE: No idea myself

OWEN: I'll text you once I arrive tomorrow

KYLE: Thx

    Kyle decided not to text Lauren as he now knew she'd be arriving sometime tomorrow. The only person left to text was Erica.

KYLE: Hey Erica, do you know when you'll be getting to Dave's house?

ERICA: I'm still on pace to be there tomorrow. My flight gets in around 5 p.m. I wasn't able to get an earlier flight

KYLE: Sounds great!

ERICA: I'll rent a car and meet you at Dave's house

KYLE: Do you want one of us to pick you up instead?

ERICA: I appreciate that, but I want to rent a car so I can drive around and see some places I haven't seen in years. I want to reminisce.

KYLE: I understand

ERICA: I'll send you a text when I land tomorrow

KYLE: TTYL

OWEN: I haven't booked a hotel yet. I might need to book one once I get there

KYLE: Sounds good. You can always stay at Dave's house

OWEN: I'll think about it

KYLE: Cool

OWEN: See you tomorrow

    Kyle was glad for the update, but it wasn't what he wanted. Not getting any response from Alex was really bothering him. It seemed that both Lauren and Owen might've been correct about Alex not being very trustworthy.

    Kyle rubbed his eyes and looked up at the flight information screen. His flight would be boarding in forty minutes. If the flight did leave at its predicted time, Kyle would still probably make it to the train station when Alex hopefully arrived.

    When Kyle finally made it onto the plane, he checked his phone one last time. Still no messages from Alex. He put his phone on flight mode with a sigh.

    "Nervous flyer? Don't worry, dear; the flight will be fine," said the kind old lady sitting beside him.

    Kyle smiled. It wasn't the flight he was nervous about.

Arrival

As soon as the plane touched down, he turned his phone back on to see there were texts from four different people.

OWEN: I got a weird call from Alex. He was not on a train at that time. He said that he'd meet me tomorrow. He also said that he wasn't sure how he'd get to Illinois. I thought he was taking a train?

    Kyle's head spun.

KYLE: Yes, he's supposed to be on the train now. Did you ask him why he said that?
OWEN: No, I wanted to make sure I was correct first. Should I text him back?

    Kyle looked at his other texts, and none of them were from Alex. There were some from Erica and two from his partners at the law firm.

As soon as Kyle was about to pull out of the airport car rental area, he received a new text.

OWEN: No answer from Alex
KYLE: No surprise. He texted Erica too for money for the train
OWEN: What a loser. Sorry to say it, but that's what he is
KYLE: No comment
OWEN: You know he is. If he doesn't respond, I guess we continue without him
KYLE: I'll be pissed off if he breaks his promise to Dave
OWEN: Same here.

Kyle's hands started sweating. He wondered if inviting Alex would be worth it. It was what Dave wanted, but on the other hand, he might've counted Alex out if he'd known there'd be this much trouble.

Since the train station was on the way to Woodbrook, Kyle would go there and wait to see if Alex showed up. His train would be arriving within the next ten minutes or so.

Kyle took the side streets and made it to the station before the train. The sun was setting, and it was a crisp eighty degrees out. No one was around, so he parked in the temporary parking spot. Two minutes later, the train pulled into the station. Kyle kept a close eye on everyone getting off the train. His total count was only six people. None of them was Alex.

"Why the fuck were you not on the train!" Kyle said to himself and then rolled down the window to cool down.

After the train started up again and was out of sight, Kyle decided to call Alex from the car.

After nine rings, no voicemail came up. Kyle hung up and slammed his hand on the dashboard. "You're an unreliable jackass!"

When his hands stopped hurting, he sent a new text.

KYLE: Where are you? I'm here for you at the station. Pick up!

After no response, Kyle figured he'd stay around for thirty minutes or so. Maybe Alex had caught the next train. As he waited, he noticed the bar across the tracks adjacent to an alley. It was one that he and Alex hid behind as kids. They'd often ding-dong-ditch people's houses when they were in their teens. One time, a cop followed them, but they'd shaken him off by hiding in that alley. It was a much simpler time for both Kyle and Alex.

Once 8:35 p.m. hit, Kyle said to himself, "I guess that you'll contact me if you need me, Alex. I can't wait around forever."

Kyle pulled out of the parking lot and headed for Dave's house.

The House

Dave's house looked a little bit different than how Kyle remembered it. The front porch flooring looked like it had been replaced. The roof looked new, as it was a reddish color now. He thought it had been brown years ago, but he wasn't entirely sure. The biggest difference was a new balcony that was now over the porch. That balcony could be accessed from Dave's old room on the second floor.

After parking on the side of the street, Kyle got out and went over to the side of the house. When he was a teenager, there had been a treehouse. The six of them were together only once up there. It was a time he would never forget. It was the time they formed the Fremont Treehouse Club.

Once he walked to the side of the house, he saw the treehouse was still there. Nothing about it looked different from what he could see from the street. It was maybe fifteen feet by ten feet, and the original wooden planks on the side were still there. The original board nailed to the tree to serve as a ladder was also still there. The detached garage and driveway were also still there near the treehouse. Kyle planned to go up there and check it out once he was settled in the house.

Before going to the porch to look for the key, he moved his car to the driveway. The garage was separate, and it had room for two cars in it, and two cars on the apron. If planned correctly, all four of their cars would fit if Owen decided to stay.

While walking up the steps to the porch, he worried that the key wouldn't be in the flowerpot. He imagined that someone local had taken it and robbed the house. He also considered that Alex might have beaten him to the house and made himself at home. As soon as Kyle spotted the flowerpot near one of the Adirondack chairs, he rushed over to it and looked inside. Luckily, the key was there. He sighed with relief.

Before opening the door, he turned around and looked across the street. An older man was entering his house. If it was the same man that lived there years ago, then it was Mr. Walsh. He'd often scold Kyle and other kids for walking on this lawn. Kyle thought Mr. Walsh had a wife, but he didn't remember ever seeing her.

Two doors to the left of Mr. Walsh's house had lived Kyle's old friend, Simon Park. They'd gone to junior high together, but Simon had gone to a private high school. The two of them had drifted apart soon after that. Simon's parents wanted him to be a doctor, so Kyle figured that was the path he'd taken.

The Greer family had once lived in the house to the left of the Park's house. They were in that house until Kyle was in fifth.

Dave told Kyle that one night, the police were there, and within a week, the whole family was gone. Kyle never got an answer as to why they left. He once asked his mother about it, and she said no one knew. Kyle felt that she'd known but hadn't wanted to tell him. It had been at least a decade since Kyle had thought about that family. When he had some spare time, he thought, he'd google them up to see what he could find.

As soon as Kyle put the key in the lock to Dave's house, he heard a voice behind him.

"So, is Mr. Fremont no longer living here?"

Kyle turned around and saw a blonde-haired boy standing on the sidewalk in front of Dave's house. He looked around fifteen or sixteen years old. He wore khaki shorts and a black collared shirt. For some reason, he had an ax in his right hand. The head of the ax was hanging down towards the ground.

"Do you mean David Fremont?"

"Yes, I was supposed to chop down one of his small trees. I talked to him about four weeks ago, and I never got around to it. He sent me some money via Paypal, so I owe him the work. I know it's almost completely dark, but I haven't had time to do this until now."

"Oh, so that's what the ax is for," Kyle said.

The boy gave a slight chuckle. "Yes, I guess I look strange walking around like this. I should've thought of that."

"Dave recently passed away, I'm afraid. I'm here to tie up all his loose ends and fulfill a promise that me and my friends made."

"Sorry to hear about that. I had no idea, Mister."

"It was a shock to many of us."

"What promise was that?" the boy asked.

"It's a secret," Kyle replied. "From a long time ago. We were probably around your age."

"I'm seventeen," the boy said.

"Well, we were a little younger than that when we made that promise."

"I'm Tim Oates. What's your name?"

"Kyle Brighton. Nice to meet you."

"Likewise, Mr. Brighton."

Tim pointed the ax at a tree on Dave's lawn. It was a tree that was no wider than a foot in circumference. Most of its leaves were gone, so it looked dead. It was a real eyesore. After Kyle nodded, Tim walked over to the tree.

"What happened to Mr. Fremont?"

"Cancer from what I heard. You didn't know about any of that?"

Tim started to chop all the branches off the tree. "He called me on the phone about a month ago. He sounded fine. I hadn't seen him in person for a few months. He kept to himself. I heard his parents died a few years back, and he inherited the house."

"I hadn't heard from him in years. We used to be great friends. There were a few of us who used to hang around this house in our teens. One of them, Simon Park, lived down the street," Kyle said.

Tim had finished with the branches, and now started to chop at the base. Kyle thought a shovel would be needed, but it wasn't. Tim chopped at the roots and the ground around it and was able to lift the tree out of the ground. He put it in a plastic bad immediately afterwards.

"This tree is completely dead. Even its roots are weak. I'll leave the few remaining roots. I'm impressed that I didn't need more than this ax to get rid of this," Tim said.

"I was thinking the same thing, Tim."

"So you used to live around here, Mr. Brighton?"

Kyle pointed to the west of the house. "I lived about a mile that way. I moved out a long time ago. My parents are no longer there, either."

"By the public pool?" Tim asked.

"Yes, a block from there. It was called Flint Pool." Kyle replied.

"I used to go to Flint a lot when I was a kid. It isn't as popular now that there's an indoor pool a few miles away. I've heard rumors that they may get rid of Flint and build some condos there."

"That's a shame," Kyle said.

"It is. I do like living in this town."

"Nothing lasts forever, Tim. I hate to say that, but it's true."

After all the remnants of the tree were put in the same bag as the tree, Tim started to walk away.

"I'll be here at least a week, Tim. If there's anything else that Dave wanted you to do, please do so. One of his relatives is taking over his house soon. If you see them, they might need some other groundskeeping done."

"Thank you, Mr. Brighton. See you around."

After Tim was gone, Kyle thought about how he used to know someone named Matt Oates. He'd lived two blocks away from Dave's house. Matt was probably seven to eight years older than Kyle. He hadn't been a nice guy, and he'd teased Kyle and Owen when they were younger. He'd often ride his car past them when they were walking home and yell at them. Both Kyle and Owen would run and hide behind bushes. If Matt was Tim's father, Tim probably got his manners from his mother.

After Kyle opened the front door, the scent of hardwood flooring in the hallway filled him with nostalgia. When he was younger, most of the house had carpet, but the area by the front door didn't. Mrs. Fremont always scolded anyone who came into the house without taking off their shoes. After taking a closer look at the flooring, he noticed it looked new, possibly less than a year old.

Past the hallway was a small room with a flatscreen TV and a small leather couch. That room used to have a small table with several vases on it. To the right of that room was a den that had a Steinway piano and two beige couches. Near the couches were some cherry oak shelves filled with books. The books looked more than a hundred years old, and were clearly just for show, as they'd likely fall apart. He picked one of them up and opened it. One of the pages instantly ripped, so he put it back right away. At the far end of the room was a fireplace. Perched on it was a silver urn. It had to be Dave's ashes. Kyle didn't know what Dave wanted to be done with the ashes yet. It was possible that one of the others knew. He took a closer look at the urn and Dave's initials was on it.

Kyle continued down the hall and arrived at the kitchen. The same brown rustic table used for dinner was still there. Kyle had never actually had dinner there, but he remembered a pizza party that Dave had in junior high. It might've been during the Super Bowl, but he couldn't remember.

After walking through the kitchen, he saw the two bedrooms on the first floor. The one on the right was Dave's parent's room, and the one on the left was a guest bedroom. Kyle didn't remember anyone ever staying in there. All he remembered was that it had a bunk bed and a dresser. He took a quick peek inside; it still had both the bunk bed and dresser. Maybe Erica and Lauren might stay in that room.

He went upstairs to see if that was still the same. The hallway up there was now filled with bamboo flooring. He distinctly remembered there had previously been a navy-blue carpet. One time he and Dave had snuck wine from the bar in the basement and had accidentally spilled it on that carpet. To cover it up, they'd taken some grape juice from the fridge and poured it over the wine stain. Dave's mother didn't notice it had been wine, but she had still been mad that the carpet was stained. Dave hadn't been allowed to have any more drinks upstairs except for water.

The upstairs had three bedrooms; one on the left, one center, and one right of the stairs. The one on the right was Dave's old room. The other two had belonged to Dave's sisters, Marie, and Vanessa. Kyle didn't know where Marie was nowadays, but he knew that Vanessa had died in a car accident a few months after Dave had graduated high school. It had been all over the local news. On a rainy night, three cars had collided. Two other people had died, and one had been in a coma. They'd died two days later.

Kyle wanted to see what was in Dave's room. The door was closed, so Kyle opened it. The room looked the same as it had in their teenage years. It was as if it had been frozen in time. There were a few movie posters such as *Top Gun* and *Goodfellas* on the walls, a clock stuck at 11:34, and a queen-sized bed with a matching chest of drawers on each side of it.

It would be a perfect place for Kyle to sleep, but he also didn't want to change anything in the room. Keeping it perfectly frozen in time would leave Dave's legacy the way that Kyle remembered it. The bed was perfectly made, and he felt it should always stay that way. As teens, they'd spent a good amount of time in there. After closing his eyes for a few seconds, he started to hear non-distinct chatter that he felt was both him and Dave. They'd had many conversations in the room about many things, all equally important in his mind. These conversations included girls, high school, and sports. After opening his eyes, the chatter was gone.

After thinking about which room to sleep in, he decided that Dave's parent's room would be best. He liked that it was the biggest and on the first floor, so he could probably hear if someone entered the house.

"I'm glad that we were friends," Kyle said aloud.

Once Kyle was done looking around Dave's room, he left and close the door behind him. There was still the basement to look at, but he figured that'd be a good place to look over once some the others arrived. It would be better to reminisce and share his feelings with someone else. Now, all he could do was wait for them to arrive.

Waiting Around

Kyle sat in the little room with the flatscreen TV he'd seen when he'd first entered the house. The remote control was missing. He eventually found it stuck between the couch cushions. The TV only had basic cable, so he soon got bored. There was no DVD player attached.

His stomach rumbled, so he went into the kitchen. The refrigerator was mostly empty except for a few bottles of cranberry and cherry juice. In the cabinets were some cans of baked beans, spaghetti and meatballs, tuna in water, and SPAM. He didn't like the choices, but his stomach was rumbling, so he had to choose something. In the end, he chose spaghetti and meatballs. As he heated it in the microwave, he found some bottled water.

It was 9 p.m. by the time he'd finished his meal. His phone buzzed with a new text message.

OWEN: I'll be there around noon tomorrow. That's the quickest I could get there
KYLE: Awesome
OWEN: Is anyone else there?

KYLE. Nope. Not even Alex. Don't know where he is

OWEN: Figures

KYLE: Don't know if he'll even show up

OWEN: We'll still fulfill our promise if he bails on us

KYLE: That's not really what we promised, but we may have to

OWEN: It's better than nothing

KYLE: I guess

OWEN: A promise is a promise

KYLE: Correct

    It was dark outside, and Kyle's eyes were dry from his contact lenses. After throwing some water on his eyes, he put his phone on charge and went into the piano room. A few framed pictures lined the bookshelf, and two were on top of the piano. There was also an unframed polaroid sitting on a bookshelf. It was of him, Alex, Dave, and another kid named Felix at a park about two blocks from the house. All four of them were on the swings. They were probably seven or eight at the time.

    Despite it being dark outside, Kyle wanted to go and visit the park. The picture had sparked a sense of nostalgia in him. He hoped that it was still there, and it hadn't been bulldozed to make way for houses. Before he left, he grabbed his cellphone and the key.

The neighborhood was tranquil as Kyle strolled past the many houses he had seen in his youth. One house particularly stuck out to him. One of his other friends, Mike Porter, lived in the small red brick house on the way to the park. It was now gone and replaced with a typical McMansion that no longer had a backyard and barely had a front lawn. Kyle remembered being in that small house once for a cub scout meeting. After passing the McMansion, he saw two more similar residences that replaced smaller houses. As much as he admired vintage houses, he was glad that those two had been replaced. He remembered them years ago as being small starter houses that had cheap aluminum siding on them.

After making a left turn around the block, he could see the park. The large metal slide was now gone. In its place was a plastic tube slide. The metal jungle gym was also gone, replaced by a plastic house with two ladders on each side. It was maybe four feet off the ground and looked dull compared to the old jungle gym. The ground around the equipment was no longer woodchips, but an ugly rubbery, multi-colored surface. As Kyle got closer to the park, he saw that the same swing set was still there. It was the only equipment that still had woodchips under it.

No one was in the park as Kyle arrived. When he was in junior high, older teenagers often hung around smoking in the evenings. There was a time when one of them chased him and

Dave out of the park. Kyle didn't know who the teenager was, and it took Kyle a few months to return to the park.

Beyond the park, Kyle could see his high school, Woodbrook South. An extra building had been added to the school, but it wasn't clear what it was. The school didn't have a swimming pool or a theatre for plays when he'd been there, so it might be either of those. He hoped to visit and see if anything else had changed.

After looking around the playground area, he sat on the farthest swing on the left side. There were six altogether, and he remembered that one being his favorite.

"I guess no one can ever go back," he said to himself, getting up. He was too large for the swing, and the chains dug into his hips.

He looked at a dirt patch at the outer edge of the park. He remembered something being there but couldn't remember what. After closing his eyes and thinking hard, it came to him. There had been a metal merry-go-round there. Local kids had named it the merry-go-round of death. It was the scariest piece of equipment in the whole park. Kids would often fall off as it spun so fast, throwing them out at high speed. Or they'd bump their heads on the safety bars. Only the bravest would try it, and Kyle wasn't one of them. He wanted to try it one time but saw some random kid stumble and hit her head on the ground from dizziness.

Just like with the merry-go-round, he'd been afraid of many things. Rollercoasters, ziplining, and swimming in the deep end of the pool were a few of his childhood fears. He'd eventually overcome them all, wondering why they'd scared him in the first place.

He looked back at the school and the new square building he'd noticed earlier. It stood on what had been an open parking lot that led to the fieldhouse where they'd often had school dances. In his junior year, he took a girl named Holly Gianetti to Homecoming, and it wasn't as enjoyable as he had hoped. He had wanted to take Lauren, but someone had already asked her two days before he had. It was the only time he'd left any of the dances early. He'd left Holly there alone, and he later regretted it.

"I'm sorry, Holly," Kyle said to himself.

Kyle kicked the woodchips and watched them spray across the grass. If he could go back and change that night, he would.

"Do all Ohio men talk to themselves?" a familiar voice asked.

A brief chill went down his spine. He looked behind him and felt very happy to see her.

"I am," she said, creating trails in the woodchips with her foot. "I don't miss him at all. He had some good points, but the cheating was something that I couldn't deal with."

Kyle wanted to ask her if she was single but couldn't quite do it. He wanted to play it cool.

"It's difficult to stay married in this day and age. At least half of my friends in Ohio are divorced," Kyle said.

"That sounds about right, Kyle. Both of my neighbors are divorced, and so is Kevin, my brother. He met a girl who just wanted to get her citizenship. She left him a few months after she got it. They had no kids, so it worked for her."

"That sucks for Kevin. He was always nice. Did he find anyone else?"

Lauren shook her head. "No, he didn't. It has been two years and nothing since."

"As I mentioned on the phone, I'm not married," Kyle said.

"Dating anyone?" she asked.

Now Kyle had the chance to ask her. "I'm not. Are you dating anyone?"

Lauren held on tightly to the swing chain. "I'm not. Like I said on the phone, I thought I had a good one, and he ruined me."

"I'm sorry," Kyle said.

He was sorry but was also glad that she was single. Asking her for a date didn't seem like an appropriate thing to do now, though. He needed to change the subject.

"I haven't heard from Alex since earlier today. He was supposed to have taken the train here. I bought him a ticket and everything. I'm very disappointed in him."

"Alex is very irresponsible. Owen told me this. I heard that he skipped out on child support payments."

"What! Alex told me he didn't have any kids. If he skipped out on payments, he's definitely not trustworthy."

Lauren looked up at the sky. Kyle wondered if she was even listening to him. Eventually, she spoke. "I'm not sure anyone is trustworthy. I feel like my life hasn't turned out the way I thought it would. I met a guy about a year ago, and he turned out to be a dud. That actually hit me harder than my divorce. A big disappointment."

"Why's that?"

"Sometimes you have expectations that are so great, and when they fail, you fall hard. This guy seemed perfect. Of course, that was the mask he wore. I know many people do that, but this was unexpected."

"Want to tell me about it?" Kyle felt surprised at how much he cared about her. He felt more than sorry for Lauren. Like her pain was his.

"He seemed to have everything: money, stability, charm. His name was Mark Grennan. Money isn't really that important, but he lied about being financially stable. I need someone who at least knows how to balance their checkbook. He was in so much debt, and he wanted me to loan him money. After he found out that I wouldn't, he became distant."

"I'm sorry to hear that." Kyle was sad that Lauren had gotten her heartbroken by this pig, but he wasn't sorry that it hadn't worked out.

"Thank you," she said. "Mark wanted everyone to believe he was loaded. He had a one hundred-thousand-dollar car. He also had a house that was worth at least half a million dollars. I've known people like him before. They like to make others think they have lots of money. They need to keep up the charade so they can make others jealous. They'd rather die than people know the truth."

Kyle had known people like that before. "They let other people's opinions shape their own lives."

"Exactly!"

"I guess the best thing to do is to forget about that guy, Lauren."

She stood and walked towards the new plastic slide. Kyle wondered if he had said something wrong. Just before he could speak, she turned around and looked him in the eye.

"Do you remember when we were at Homecoming, and you left early?"

He felt dizzy. "I was just thinking about that a few minutes before you snuck up on me."

"Why did you leave that night? Owen said you left early for some reason. Holly was still there when you left." "Do you want to know the truth, Lauren?"

"I wouldn't have it any other way, Kyle."

He paused for a few seconds until he knew what to say. "It was because I wanted to be there with you. I feel bad for leaving her there, but I was not with the girl that I wanted to be with. Don't you remember I asked you, but you already had a date?"

Her smirk couldn't be hidden. "I do remember. I wish that you'd asked me earlier. Brent Fargo asked me two days before you did. He was a total bore when I was there. He ignored me a lot of the night. He apologized later. We also went to prom together. He acted better at prom, but I didn't have as good as I wanted. My mind was partly on you, Kyle."

Kyle tried to stop blushing and looked down at the woodchips. "I wish that I'd asked you earlier. Holly wasn't much fun, either. She was a beautiful girl, but there was nothing interesting about her. She took advantage of the fact that her parents had money. She had a brand-new Camaro when she was sixteen and always had the nicest clothes."

"Did you not like Holly?"

The truth was that Kyle didn't like her at all. She was more popular than Lauren, but most people hung around her because they enjoyed her lifestyle. She often had parties with alcohol and loud music in her big house. Dozens of people showed up, and no one ever called the police. Kyle had been to a few of those parties and never felt like he fit in.

"I didn't like her much. I know she broke up with her boyfriend a short time before Homecoming, so she needed someone quickly. I feel like I shouldn't have gone."

"I heard how Holly turned out," Lauren said with a bigger smirk than before.

"Do tell."

Lauren sat back on the swing. "I heard that she married some guy who had more money than she did. After a few years, the guy lost most of his wealth on real estate gone bad. She divorced him within a year."

"I guess that's karma," Kyle said.

"She also looks ten years older than she really is. I saw her on Facebook a few weeks ago. She would mock other girls in high school for not having perfect skin like she had. Like you said, karma."

"What goes around, comes around, I guess. I wonder if she regrets acting that way."

Lauren started to swing back and forth. "I doubt she's truly sorry for her attitude. She'd probably only say she was sorry if it got her sympathy."

"I bet you're right."

Kyle started to swing too. He thought about how lucky he was that Lauren had met him in the park when she did. If Alex had been here, the conversation would've been different.

"I'm enjoying this, Lauren. I feel like I've gone back in time. I used to hang out here when I was a kid."

Lauren stopped swinging. "I'm glad that you brought Homecoming up."

"What about it?"

"Did you know I came to look for you after you left Homecoming?" Lauren asked.

Kyle stopped swinging as well. "I didn't know that." His heart started to beat faster.

"Holly told me you'd left, so I went outside to see if you were by that patio that's now where the new pool is." She pointed to the square building that Kyle had noticed a few minutes.

"I wondered what that building was for," Kyle said.

"I read about it on Facebook about a year ago. They also replaced all the lockers. My senior year, I remember having #1896."

Kyle wondered if he'd even recognize the inside of the school now. His favorite areas had been the cafeteria, library, and the commons at the far end of the building. He imagined they all probably had flat-screen TVs in them now and weren't peaceful like they used to be.

"I may go in there if I can before I leave."

"If I'm around still, let's go together."

It hit him that Lauren would only be around for a few days before returning home. He wanted to get to know her more.

"I'm glad that you're here," he said.

"Likewise," she said, smiling.

A buzz came from his cellphone. He pulled it from his pocket.

ERICA: I'll be arriving at 10:35 tomorrow morning. Has anyone else arrived there yet?
KYLE: Just Lauren
ERICA: Nice! Enjoy your time with her

Kyle wondered what she meant by that last text. It didn't seem like something she'd normally comment on. It was as if she knew something about Lauren that he didn't.

KYLE: Do you mean something by that last comment?

ERICA: Just that it's nice that the two of you are alone

KYLE: Why?

ERICA: Enjoy it while you can. You won't be alone for long

"Anyone from our group?" Lauren asked.

"Yes, Erica. She'll be here tomorrow," Kyle replied, grinning.

"Will everyone be here by tomorrow, then?"

Kyle figured that Owen would arrive by tomorrow, but he wasn't sure about Alex. He might be in Woodbrook already in a dive bar, or he could still be in Milwaukee.

"The only one that I'm not sure about is Alex. Like I said, we haven't spoken since earlier today. Once this is all over, I doubt I'll ever contact him again. He said he'd be here, so I bought him a train ticket. Unless he's hurt and can't contact us. I can't think of any other good excuse for him not telling us where he is."

"I sense some hostility there, Kyle."

She was correct. Kyle was now at a point where he didn't have any sympathy for Alex. He recognized the type of person Alex was. When Kyle was a sophomore in college, he had a roommate who was always asking others for money. Once, he borrowed five-hundred dollars from Kyle and never gave it back. There was always an excuse, no matter how lame it sounded. Kyle found a new roommate for the rest of his sophomore year.

"Sorry, but I've had people in my life like Alex. They're users, plain and simple. They can't really be counted on. From talking to you and the others, Alex still seems to have a reputation for being unreliable. I don't need anyone like that in my life."

"I do know what you mean, Kyle. I just think you need to look past that until we know what's really going on. There may be something deeper to him that we don't know about. We need to all get together like we promised Dave and forget our differences until we accomplish what we said we would."

Kyle knew she was right. He didn't want to feel that way about Alex. Deep inside, he knew he needed to give him a chance. Hopefully, all that resentment would disappear once the five of them were together again.

"You're right. I'll see what his story is," Kyle said. He held his hand out to Lauren.

She put her hand in his. "I'm always here for you."

Kyle wanted to pull her closer so that he could kiss her, but the fear of rejection held him back. He received another text and instinctively moved his hand to read the message.

ERICA: She liked you in high school. You knew that, right?

Kyle couldn't hold in his smile. He looked down at the woodchips.

KYLE: How about now?

ERICA: I don't know. You should try and find out

KYLE: I'll try

There was no more waiting. He pulled Lauren towards him and kissed her. She kissed him back. After a moment, they separated, staring at each other.

"I can't believe that just happened. I feel like I'm in heaven," Kyle said.

"I've wanted that ever since we were in high school."

The two of them stood and embraced. Kyle wanted to stay that way all night. He wasn't going to let go first.

Catching Up

Eventually, Lauren let go.

"Maybe it was our luck that Alex didn't get here when he was supposed to," she said.

"You've got a good way of looking at things, Lauren."

Holding hands, they started to walk away. Kyle looked over at the high school and then looked back at Lauren. Do you want to check out the school grounds?"

She nodded.

As they walked towards the school, they passed near where the merry-go-round used to be.

"The merry-go-round used to be in this spot," Kyle said. "Remember how lethal that thing was?"

"I know," Lauren said as she pointed to a tiny scar below her chin. "I got this when I jumped off while it was moving. I hit my chin on a rock in the grass."

"I wish I could go back to those times," Kyle said. "Everything was much simpler with fewer worries."

"I wish for that sometimes, too. All we can do is remember what we had and hold it in our hearts. Dave's death shook me when you told me. I bawled yesterday when I got off the phone with you."

They continued to the fence surrounding the east end of the high school. The entrance to the parking lot was open. In their high school days, it was the smokers' lot. Kyle tried his first cigarette there. It was one of the worst tastes he had ever experienced.

They entered the parking lot and saw a car parked near the far end of the swimming pool building. Someone moved inside the vehicle, so he and Lauren stopped. It was clear there were two people in the car. One of them looked straight at him and turned on the car. A few seconds later, the car was out of the parking lot.

"That was fast!" Lauren remarked.

"There were two of them in there. Maybe they were making out," Kyle responded.

Lauren kissed him on the cheek. "That's something I never did."

"What? Made out in a car?"

"Exactly!" she replied. "I only had one boyfriend in high school. He was a nice guy, but we never did more than kiss. I never made out with any guy who wasn't my boyfriend. At least that was my attitude in high school."

"Was your boyfriend the guy that you went to Homecoming with?"

She nodded. "Yes, that was Brent Fargo. I also went with him to prom. He seemed super nice at the time, but he went to the Ivy League and broke up with me shortly after we graduated from high school. I saw his true colors. I'm glad he showed me his real self, as it never would've worked out. I heard he has some investment firm that made him wealthy. He's been married three times, I think."

"I guess you know that through social media. I don't know what's happened to most people, as I stay off it. I don't even know if anyone else has died, Except for Lucas...I can't remember his last name..."

"At least three that I know of. Megan Sanders, Billy Perkins, and Lucas Wright, that is the one you're thinking of. Poor Megan and Billy died in college. They both went to the University of Illinois and died in the same car crash. A drunk driver hit the car head-on. They were with another person not from our high school, and he died too. I don't know how Lucas died.

The first two people Kyle hadn't known well, but he had known Lucas well when they were younger. They'd been on the same city baseball team. Lucas was a star baseball player in high school, but he got caught with pot in his senior year, so he was kicked off the team. His lost his college baseball scholarship.

"I knew Lucas pretty well, Lauren. I didn't see him after Dave's graduation party. I wish that I'd known of his passing. I was sad when I heard he'd passed. I know what happened. It was a drug deal gone bad. At least, that's what I'd heard. He was twenty or maybe twenty-one when it happened."

"That's sad, Kyle. I never thought he would've gotten involved in something like that."

Kyle didn't want to talk about death anymore, so he gently pulled Lauren toward the pool building. When they turned the corner, they saw windows low enough for them to look inside.

'I'm glad we didn't have this pool when we went here," Lauren said.

"Why's that?"

"Because I wouldn't have looked good in a bathing suit."

Kyle grabbed her other hand and looked her straight in the eyes. "You were in perfect shape back then. You still are."

"Thank you, Kyle. I had a bad problem then and in college,"

"Care to talk about it?" He put his hand on her shoulder.

She took a deep breath. "I had a problem with bulimia. My case wasn't as bad as some other girls in our class, but it affected me. I once overheard a boy say that I was fat. That really hit me hard. I don't even remember the guy's name, but I remember his face."

Her tears continued to flow. "I want to ask you a question, and I need an honest answer."

Kyle stood up. "Of course, I'll be truthful. Ask away!"

"Do you think you would ever want to date me?"

Kyle was shocked. He thought it was obvious he would, as they had just kissed. "Yes, of course. I've liked you ever since high school. It's a miracle that we had the chance to meet like this before everyone else got here. It's like a gift from God."

She kept crying. "Oh, my God! Life can be so full of bullshit!"

Kyle didn't know what to say. He wasn't sure if she thought he was lying or if she meant something else. She turned around and started to tremble.

"I'm sorry if I said something wrong, Lauren."

"You didn't. It's me. I've made too many mistakes in the past. You're acting like the perfect gentleman. I want to date you too! I know it's been years since we've seen each other, but that old feeling never left me."

He slowly approached her. "Then why are you crying? Is there some other underlying issue?"

She took another step away. "I've got a problem that I can't tell you about right now. It'll ruin the moment. I didn't think about it until a few seconds ago. Being here with you made me forget about it. I may be able to tell you about it later."

"Okay," Kyle said. "I won't ask about it. I hope you can tell me about it another time, though. Maybe I can help you."

"There's nothing you can do," she said, shaking her head. "No one can. It's something that can't be undone."

Kyle really wanted to know what it was. Her change of mood all seemed so sudden. The past hour had been wonderful before now.

"I won't bring it up again unless you do," said Kyle. "If you want to tell me, you will."

"Please don't tell the others I have a secret. I haven't told any of them about my situation, either."

He held his hand over his heart and said, "I won't mention any of this. I can guarantee that."

"Thank you, Kyle. I believe that you'll keep that promise."

He pointed towards the park. "Do you want to go back to the park or Dave's house?"

"Let's check out the school. I don't want to disappoint you."

"We can do that another time. If you want to go back to the house, let's do that. There'll be other days to check out the grounds around here."

Kyle suddenly remembered the ashes. "On another note, I was told that Dave believed one of us would know what to do with his ashes. I don't. Do you?"

"I don't know. I can't think of anything right now. I'm very tired."

"I understand, Lauren."

She approached him and held out her hand. Their hands locked again but only for a few second as she let go. Kyle felt a bit uneasy about the situation. This secret was going to bother him for the next few days. He hoped she'd tell him what it was. If she didn't, he would just need to accept not knowing.

Walking Back

Kyle and Lauren walked back towards Dave's house side-by-side. Kyle's stomach started to bother him. Despite Lauren saying that he'd done nothing wrong, he had an underlying feeling he had. Something he'd said might've triggered their time together go south.

"When we get back, do you want to go to sleep?" Kyle asked.

She nodded. "I want to. However, I may not be able to. This problem is now on my mind. If you knew what it was, you would realize there's nothing I can do about it."

"I just want to ask one thing about that. Does it have anything to do with me?"

Her hands clenched together as if she was trying to hold something in. "Yes and no. Please don't ask about it right now. I don't want you to be disappointed. That's the gist of it. The problem is all on me, and I don't know how to explain my situation. I need to explain it in a way you'll understand. It may make you not want to date me anymore. That's all I'll say about it right now."

"How do you know I wouldn't want to date you anymore?"

"Please, let's drop this for the moment, Kyle. Maybe we can talk about it in a few days. After our time here is over, you still want to keep in touch, right?"

"Yes, no matter what the issue is, we still will. I don't think anything would make me not want to date you, Lauren. Maybe you won't like *me* after you get to know me."

"Now, what could you possibly do to make me dislike you, Kyle?"

Kyle didn't want to be negative about himself, but bragging didn't seem right either. "I don't think there'll be anything, but different people want different things."

"That's part of my problem," she said. "I think there's something about me that you won't like. One of my past adult boyfriends didn't like this thing.'"

"I do want to know what this is about, but I respect that you need to tell me how and when you want to. It seems very important to you, and I respect that."

"Thank you, Kyle."

His body tingled all over; she had that effect on him. It was like being back in the corridors of high school again. He enjoyed having a crush like he did in high school. It definitely was childish, but he knew that didn't matter. After high school, he had forgotten that feeling. Having it back was a blessing.

To lighten up the mood, he smiled and said, "Next subject."

They were close to Dave's house, so Kyle looked around and saw Simon Park's house again. "Do you know what Simon wound up doing with his life?"

She smiled back. "Actually, I do. He was going to be a doctor but got in trouble in college. I don't know the whole story, but he went into the Marines to straighten himself out. I think he's a major. He's out near San Diego now, I believe. He had a few pics up on Instagram a few years back of him with his wife and two kids. I never knew him all that well, but I know you did."

"Speaking of Simon, I know that the Greer's used to live by him. They left their house in a hurry. Do you know why that happened?"

"I do know why, Kyle. At least I think I do. The dad of that family was involved in some crimes. Cops raided the house one night."

"That's crazy," Kyle said. "At least Simon's family was not like that. You seem to know a lot about the neighborhood."

"I used to speak with others that lived around here, Kyle. Lots of gossip. That stopped over the years. I didn't get to know Simon that well, but I only heard good things about him."

"Yes, he was a good friend," Kyle said. "His parents were very strict, though. He wanted to go with us on that long walk we all took that one rainy November day, but they wouldn't let him. It was the Sunday after Thanksgiving. Do you remember that day?"

"Yes, I do. I believe that was the last time all six of us were together; you, me, Dave, Alex, Erica, and Owen. It was in our sophomore year of high school, I think. I was trying to get to know more about you. Despite everyone being there, we had a good conversation."

Kyle was amazed she remembered all that. That had been one of the best days of his life.

"I'm glad you remember it, Lauren. We were all so young. Just two months later, Owen got his license, so he started hanging out with a few others. Other people latched on to him for rides. I think one of them was a guy named Glen. I spent some time with Owen later on in class, but it was never the same."

Lauren looked at her cellphone and yawned. "I didn't like that. He was always too busy. It was like his license changed his life. I even asked him for a ride one time, and he said he couldn't. I did this without my mother knowing that I asked him. She probably would've flipped if she knew that I asked a boy to drive me anywhere. I guess, luckily, he said no so that situation never needed to be discovered by my mom. His excuse was that he had some homework to do. I later found out that he was hanging around with Glen Scherner that day. He flat-out lied to me. I don't care about that now, but I did then."

Kyle remembered Glen. He had gotten kicked out of school in his senior year. The rumor was that he'd brought a gun to school. He had slicked-back brown hair and often pounced at younger students to frighten them. He never hurt them, so there was no punishment.

"That's a guy who probably turned out bad in life," Kyle said.

Lauren giggled. "He did. Glen was caught trying to steal electronics at a local Walmart a few years after getting kicked out of school. That was just the beginning. He was later part of some crime ring that broke into trucks. I hear he's still in jail."

"You seem to know a lot about what's happened to the people around here," Kyle said. "I'm amazed. I barely know anything about anyone."

"It's a double-edged sword," she said. "You get to keep in touch with or rediscover old friends, but you get people bragging about their lives, or at least giving what they want people to think their life is."

They both stopped by Dave's front porch. Lauren gave a coy smile like she wanted to kiss him again. His hands shook in anticipation.

"Is there a room for me?"

"I'll be sleeping in his parent's old room. I want to leave Dave's room as it is. You can take your pick of the other rooms. The room across from me has a bunkbed. Upstairs are Vanessa's and Marie's rooms. I'm not sure if they have beds in them or not."

"If they don't, I can use one of the bunks or a couch."

"As long as you're comfortable and get a good night's sleep."

Lauren went to her car and took her suitcase out of the trunk. She then walked up the steps onto the deck. After getting to the door, she turned around and looked up at the sky before looking at Kyle. He couldn't tell if she was happy or sad.

"You've shown me something about you," she said.

The back of his neck started to sweat.

"What did I show you?" he asked.

"You didn't ask me to go to your room. Most men would have."

Kyle's heart started to beat fast. "I want to get to know you again. I have the best intentions."

"I know you do. You were that way when we were young. I was afraid you'd lost that quality. Many people do. I'm going inside now. Are you going inside?"

"I'll go inside in a few minutes. Have a good night, Lauren. I'll be up around 8 am. Maybe we can go for breakfast or something like that?"

"That sounds great! Wake me up in time. I'll look around the house now and pick a room."

She disappeared into the house. He stood on the porch and looked up at the stars, thinking about that one rainy November day the six of them had shared. Despite it being such a fun day, he hadn't thought of that day in years. They were all so young and full of hope. If he could relive any day from his youth, that'd be the one.

November of 1995

Kyle, Alex, and Dave waited on the front porch. Owen was late as usual. According to Dave, Erica and Lauren were possibly coming along too. Kyle hadn't talked to either of the two girls since late summer. Erica went to a private school, and Lauren had seen him in the halls, but all she did was smile or nod. Her smile was refreshing. He wished she would smile at him more often.

As usual, Alex was listening to his CD Walkman while Dave kept looking at his wristwatch. Kyle wished they'd talk more. Silence made him uncomfortable.

"What time did you tell Owen to get here?" Kyle asked Dave.

"I told him to be here by 10 a.m. He's fifteen minutes late."

Alex pulled off his headphones. "Kyle the Pile, I don't care if Owen comes. I just want the two girls to come along. Erica is cute."

Kyle had never thought about Erica like that. He hadn't talk to her much the last time they'd been together, and she seemed to enjoy talking to Owen the most."

"She didn't really talk to most of us last time. She did seem interested in Owen, though. Sorry, Alex."

"Not interested in her," Alex said. "I was just humoring her. She doesn't have what I want."

"What do you mean?" Kyle asked.

"She should see a dermatologist," Alex joked.

"Alex, I thought you said Erica was cute. Were you joking?" Kyle asked.

Alex rolled his eyes. "I course I was, Pile. Couldn't you hear the sarcasm in my voice? Owen can have her. Lauren is the cute one."

Kyle didn't like how Alex talked unkindly about Erica with such ease. Alex himself wasn't exactly a hit with the girls, but it wasn't Kyle's style to mention it. He knew Alex was talking bad about Erica because she liked Owen, not him.

"Lauren is cute," Dave said as he ran his hand through his brown hair. "I heard she has a boyfriend, though. I didn't ask her to bring him along. He'd be a third wheel."

"What do you think of Lauren?" Alex asked Kyle.

It wasn't an easy question for Kyle. He thought she was pretty but didn't want to sound keen. The truth was he harbored some feelings for her but hadn't gotten to know her much. He wasn't sure if she was just a good-looking girl with no personality.

"She's cute. I haven't really talked to her since we were in the treehouse that night. She always dresses well, and she's probably the prettiest blonde in our whole class."

"So you like Lauren?" Alex quipped.

Kyle blushed, so he looked at his feet. "I don't know yet."

"Don't worry, Pile. I won't say anything. I don't think she likes me. I pissed her off a few weeks ago in gym class."

"What happened?" Kyle asked.

"I mentioned that she had nice legs and that she's a tease. Also, I told her that her gym shorts weren't tight enough for her ass. She told Mr. Phelps what I'd said. I thought I was going to get a detention, but he just told me to stop. I did stop, but I never apologized to her."

"Maybe you should," Kyle said. "It could spoil today if you don't."

"Don't go there. I don't think I need to do anything. I'm sure she'll be casual. If she isn't, it will be a quiet day between her and me."

Before Kyle could say anything more, he noticed Owen approaching the porch. He wore an open red and black flannel shirt and ripped blue jeans. He was carrying a white plastic bag.

"What's in the bag?" Kyle asked.

"It's a box of beer that I took from my parents' basement. There are six cans left, one for each of us if the two girls come along."

"Where are they, anyways? Do you know, Owen?" Dave asked.

Owen shrugged his broad shoulders. "Fucked if I know. I talked with Lauren a few days ago in geometry class. She said she'd be here by ten-thirty if she was coming along."

"And the girl with acne problems?" Alex asked.

Owen shook his head. "Jesus, Alex. Do you need to joke about anything and everything?"

"I do, Owen Sewer."

"It's Seward, not sewer! You must stop calling me that."

"Like I said, Sewer."

Owen dropped the bag on the grass. His hands were clenched into fists, and Kyle waited for him to charge Alex. Kyle knew that if Owen did charge at Alex, no one would be able to stop him. Owen was just under six feet tall and full of muscle.

"Shut up, Alex!" Dave said.

There was silence of a moment. Eventually, Owen picked up the bag of beer.

"Should we go without the girls?" Kyle asked.

Owen shook his head. "Let's wait a bit. It'll be much more fun with them."

"I agree," said Alex. "Let's wait a few more minutes. If they don't have the courtesy to be here soon, screw them." It was as if Alex was trying to agree with Owen to smooth things over.

Dave pointed across the street to Simon's house. "What about Simon? Is he coming?"

"Forget about him," Alex said, rolling his eyes. "All that guy does is study. He'd bore us to death. He wasn't with us in the treehouse over the summer anyways."

"Never mind about him," Owen responded. "I spoke with him last night, and he said that it was unlikely he'd be able to sneak out past his parents."

"Yeah, just like how he couldn't join our club in the treehouse a few months ago. The guy has no social life," Alex said.

Kyle knew Simon well. They were both in advanced classes. It wasn't far off that Simon studied all the time. His parents wanted him to become a doctor. His older sister Jessica was studying for the same career. The only difference was that Simon wasn't as fast a learner as Jessica. That bothered him, so he worked twice as hard as her, yet he still didn't do as well. "I don't care if he comes," Alex said. "All that matters is whether the two girls do."

Owen sat down on the first step of the porch. "Speaking of being successful, I hope I can get into a great college for football. I'm getting mostly C grades, and I got a D in Geometry. Probably only an average college for me if I don't get a scholarship to a sports powerhouse."

"Coach Berger has been helping you, right?" Kyle asked.

"He has. I just want to make sure that I don't flunk out. I've been lucky to get the grades I have. Studying never seems to work for me."

"I can help you if you want," Kyle proposed.

"I appreciate that, Kyle. Let's set something up next week."

Just before Kyle could reply, he saw the two girls approaching the house. Lauren was wearing a blue hoodie and jeans, while Erica had her red winter jacket on, and black jeans chafed at the bottom.

"Hello, girls!" It's great to see the two of you," Alex said.

As they got closer, Kyle saw that Erica's acne had cleared up. He wondered if Alex had noticed. Lauren looked beautiful as always, and there was something different about her. Kyle couldn't make out what it was, though.

"Are we still going to Dade Woods?" Lauren asked.

"Yes," Dave said. "It's supposed to rain soon, but I want to go anyways."

"No treehouse today?" Erica asked Dave.

"Not today. This can be an FTC meeting with the treehouse. I hope we all can meet there again soon, though."

"Cool beans," Erica said.

Lauren looked at Kyle and smiled. He realized her braces were gone. Her teeth were perfectly straight, making her even better looking.

"It's nice to see both of you," Kyle said.

"Likewise," both the girls said in unison.

The boys joined the girls on the grass. Alex went straight over to Erica. Kyle hoped Alex wouldn't say anything crude to her today. A few drops of rain fell, so Owen pointed down the street toward Dade Woods. Without saying anything, everyone followed his lead.

November Rain

"I hope it doesn't start to pour," Erica said.

"Don't worry about that, Erica," Alex said with a smirk. "We've got this beautiful November rain out here."

She looked at him and then ahead as if nothing had happened.

"Lame," Dave said.

"I was mentioning it because of the song. I know that at least some of you liked it. It was my favorite during eighth grade. It was a joke I guess no one got."

Erica shook her head. "Nobody cares, Alex. Just don't start singing, okay?"

Kyle didn't know whether to laugh or feel bad for Alex. Sometimes, Kyle wanted Alex to feel self-conscious about his jokes, but this didn't seem like the time. Erica almost seemed like she was mad at Alex. Could it be that she somehow knew about Alex's remarks about her acne?

"Well, you guys are going to be boring today if you don't lighten up," Alex said.

"I've never been to Dade Woods before," Lauren said, clearly trying to change the subject.

"I was there last week with a few other people," Owen said. "We shot the shit after having a few cigs."

"You smoke?" Erica asked. "Doesn't that affect your lungs for running in football?"

Owen gave a dismissive wave and looked at the ground.

The six of them walked in pairs, making up three rows due to the narrow sidewalk. Owen and Erica were in the front, Dave and Alex were next, then Lauren and Kyle. Kyle glanced at Lauren and saw she was biting her lip.

"Everything ok, there?" Kyle asked.

She looked at Kyle. "I'm ok. I just am having some issues with my parents. They wouldn't let me go with you guys today, so I snuck out."

"I'm glad you came with us," Kyle said.

"Thanks. I need a day like this. I haven't been able to get out much."

The others had moved on a bit quicker, leaving a gap between them, Kyle and Lauren. Kyle liked that the two of them had a little space to talk.

"I never thought that the six of us would be together again," Kyle said. "That meeting we had in the treehouse was kind of fun. It's only been a few months since we were there."

"I liked it too. Dave's promise was cool. It made me feel like I was part of something. I've never really felt that I was part of anything. I was part of Girl Scouts, but my mother forced me into that. I didn't like some of the girls there."

"Yes, I liked our promise. I consider it to be a pact."

"Do you think the others will stick to it, Kyle? I know that Alex is always joking, so it may not mean much to him. To me, the circle that we formed made me feel as if no one except the six of us could make that circle go away. No one can take that away from us. Does that make sense?"

He nodded. It did make sense to Kyle. Only the six of them formed the circle, and no one else knew about it. It was like their own secret society.

"Are the two of you going to fall any further behind?" Alex called. All four of them had stopped and were waiting for Kyle and Lauren.

Owen, Alex, and Erica all turned around and kept walking. Dave stared at Kyle and Lauren for a few seconds before he joined the others. Kyle felt that Dave had a look of disgust on his face before he turned around.

"Let's catch up with them, Lauren. Dave doesn't look happy."

Kyle and Lauren caught up to them. Alex made a stupid face at them, sticking out his upper teeth like a horse.

Owen said, "We'll go down Keller Lane and cut through the hidden cemetery to get to Madsen Boulevard. Dade Woods isn't far from there."

They continued walking. Kyle and Lauren fell behind so they could talk privately again.

"Alex is so obnoxious," he said. "I think he's pissing Erica off."

"She's mad at him. She knows he's been talking shit about her for weeks. Her mom got her pills for her acne, and it's mostly gone. Alex said something to Ben Suarez about her skin. Alex didn't even know that Ben is her cousin. Ben told me, and I felt that I needed to tell her. I didn't say exactly what Alex had said, but I told her Alex had been talking shit about her."

"So nothing about her skin?"

"Nothing specific. I said it wasn't important. What was important was that she shouldn't trust him."

Kyle realized that Lauren had a great heart. She could've told Erica the exact truth, but that would have hurt her feelings.

"I'm glad you didn't tell her, Lauren. I think anyone would be insecure about such a thing."

They caught up with the others again, and the gang continued down Keller Lane until they arrived at a small field. There were two red brick houses on each side of the field. Just past the field were a few trees and tall grass. Kyle couldn't see a cemetery.

They walked in a line through the field and tall grass and shade. Owen led the way and veered to the right. Kyle saw why. Two headstones stood in the middle of all the foliage. Both tombstones had the Star of David on them. He couldn't determine the names, but one of the death dates was 1902.

"This is a strange place to have a cemetery," Dave remarked.

"I'm not really sure why it's here, but I've counted seven headstones so far," Owen said. "There used to be a fence here that blocked off the way to Madsen Boulevard."

Kyle remembered that fence. He never knew there were graves beyond it.

"I'm surprised they took down the fence," Kyle said.

"Didn't you hear?" Dave asked. "They're going to relocate all the graves to another place about ten miles from here."

Kyle shook his head. "I didn't even know what was in this area."

As they were leaving the cemetery, Kyle stopped and looked back. He thought about the few people buried there, one of them for over ninety years. It was highly unlikely that anyone alive would remember that person. He felt sad, hoping he wouldn't be forgotten and buried in such a place.

Madsen Boulevard was ahead of them. There was one stoplight and a few old buildings. One of the buildings had the year 1878 in the brickwork. A SPACE AVAILABLE sign was in the window. The next building also had the same sign. A Carter's Shoe Store was open on the opposite side of the street. Despite being less than a mile from his house, Kyle rarely went to Madsen Boulevard.

"This area has seen better times," he remarked.

"This used to be the downtown," Owen said as he looked at Erica, "but it's been a dead zone for the last few years. Pine School down the street is also gone. I used to think it was haunted. My cousin went there about ten years ago, but it was closed before I could go."   Kyle also thought it was haunted. There was a playground near it that was still around despite the school being closed. He imagined that the ghosts of dead kids haunted that playground.

"I heard they're going to bulldoze all this within the next six months," Dave said. "They'll put condos here."

Kyle thought it was sad that it would all be gone soon. The area had history, and yet it would all be erased for newer buildings.

"It's like that with the library, too," Erica said.

"For real? It's being torn down?" Kyle asked.

Erica shook her head. "It's just getting renovated. I heard it's getting a second floor and computers instead of card catalogs. Finally getting with the times!"

The six of them passed the buildings and saw Dade Woods across the street. The rain started to come down. "Let's get into the woods. It'll block some of the rain."

"I actually don't mind the rain," Dave said. "I find it peaceful."

"Who finds it peaceful?" Alex asked with a sarcastic tone.

"Piss off, Alex," snapped Dave. "You don't have to come with us today."

Alex laughed and followed the group into the trees. Kyle noticed that Alex had a bent Mark McGuire baseball card in his hand. It was one that Alex bought off Kyle. Kyle remembered Alex wanting it badly and now he was carrying it around in bad condition.

The foliage blocked most of the rain. Lauren put up her hood. Kyle wished he had a hoodie too. His brown hair fell in wet clumps, and he suspected he looked ridiculous.

"I'll break out the cigs once we get to the old oil drum," Owen said.

Lauren leaned over to Kyle and said, "I don't want to smoke. I tried it once and it hurt my throat."

Kyle had never tried it before but was curious to. "I think I might pass on it." He wanted to impress Lauren, but was afraid of what the other guys might think if he said no.

The oil drum was in a small clearing. Empty beer bottles littered the ground. Kyle noticed a cigar box too. He opened it to see that it was empty.

"So you guys were smoking cigars too, Owen?" Alex asked.

"Trent Kovacs was. Me and Glen Scherner had cigarettes."

"Hanging out with the older guys, huh?" Erica said, smirking.

Owen shrugged. "They can drive, and they also get me some of the best weed out there."

"Do you have any weed on you now?" Alex asked.

"No, I'm out. I need to get more. I just need to be careful not to get caught with it by a cop."

After pulling out a cigarette and putting it in his mouth, Owen offered one to Dave and Alex, and they both took one. After Owen lit his and blew smoke out of his nostrils, Erica put her hand out expectantly. He offered out the pack, and she took one. Once she took her first drag, she let out a cough. Kyle and Lauren were now the only ones not smoking as they stood around the oil drum. Owen stared at both, clearly waiting for them to ask for a cigarette.

"I think I'll pass on those. I tried it once and it gave me a headache," Kyle said.

"Me too," Lauren added. "I hate the way that it hurts my throat."

Alex snickered, smoke rising from his mouth in plumes. "You two are a bunch of pussies. One isn't going to hurt you. Don't be posers."

"It's my choice, fucko," said Kyle. "I don't want a bad habit."

The truth was that Kyle had never had a cigarette in his life. His parents didn't smoke, but his uncle did, and it always left a bad smell on his clothes.

Owen pulled out a small bottle of lighter fluid and poured it into the drum. Kyle looked into the drum and saw a few branches, along with an empty beer box. Owen threw a match in and set the contents ablaze. The copious amount of lighter fluid made the fire ferocious, eating away at the wood.

"It'll keep us warm if we get too cold," Owen said.

Lauren put her hands out to the flames. "It's getting kind of cold out here."

"Are you sure you don't want a cig, babe?" Alex asked Lauren.

Before Lauren could respond, Erica said. "If she wants one, she'll ask for one. You're so stupid sometimes."

"Maybe I should just forget about his shit-talking and be nice to him," said Erica. "I hope he'll change his ways, though."

Everyone nodded in agreement.

"Let's give him a few minutes," Owen said.

Owen and Dave each had another cigarette. Owen offered one to Kyle and Lauren, but they both refused. When Owen was nearly done with his cigarette, he pulled a small bottle of vodka from his pocket. Kyle had never seen such a small bottle. He doubted it would fill a small glass.

"You drink too?" Kyle asked.

"On occasions. My old man does, so I swiped one of these from the desk drawer in the basement. I'm not even sure if my mom knows about them." Owen drank the bottle in one gulp.

"Shall we go look for Alex?" Lauren asked, looking in the direction Alex had headed.

Dave smiled. "Good members of the FTC always stick together. We have some sort of comradery. It's our secret society."

Kyle took a step, the floorboard of Dave's deck creaking beneath his shoe. He breathed in the warm air, aware of Lauren moving inside Dave's house. He thought about Dave's words, soaking in what he'd said. He didn't realize that the Fremont Treehouse Club had meant so much to Dave. As a group of six, they'd only met twice, once in the treehouse and on the current walk to Dade Woods. However, it clearly affected and shaped Dave's life.

"I'll never forget that night," Kyle said. "Hopefully we can do that again."

"I would like to get together like that again too," Lauren added.

Owen threw the empty bottle into the drum. He signaled with his hand for Erica to go with him, and the two of them disappeared into the woods.

"I didn't realize that Alex was having such a hard time," Lauren said to Kyle. "I've heard some of my friends say they hate life, but they're fine the next day. Were you aware of what's been going on with him?"

"I wasn't. He's always been so goofy. I wonder how long he's been feeling like this. Do you think that Erica still likes Owen? She *did* want to go with him to find Alex."

"I think she does. She doesn't have a boyfriend right now. I think he likes her too. I caught him staring at her a few times today."

This was now the perfect time for Kyle to ask Lauren if she had a boyfriend, as Dave was busy staring into the woods after the others. Earlier that day, Dave had said that he thought she did. "What about you, Lauren?"

"Do I have a boyfriend?"

She shook her head and looked towards the ground. "I don't. Someone at school asked me if I did last week. I haven't had a boyfriend in my life. Did someone tell you that I did?"

Dave started to walk back towards them. Kyle tried not to make eye contact with him. "I was just curious. No one mentioned that you had one." He felt bad about lying, but it was just a white lie.

'What were you curious about?" Dave asked Kyle.

Kyle didn't answer but Lauren did. "Kyle asked if I had a boyfriend."

"I heard that you had one," Dave said as he smirked.

"Who told you that I had one, Dave?"

"Andy Richmond did."

"What an asshole! I barely know him," she said.

"No reason to be trippin' on it. There are always rumors going around about people. I've heard some about me from time to time," Dave said.

"What else have you heard about me, Dave?" she asked.

"Nothing," Dave replied. "That's the only thing I heard about you."

Kyle was now curious about himself. "Have either of you heard any rumors about me?"

Lauren nodded her head. "I heard you're the smartest guy in our class. I guess that might be a fact and not a rumor, though."

"Andy Richmond was ahead of me last semester in our GPAs. He's the head of the class." Kyle said to Lauren before looking to Dave.

"Anything else about me, Dave?" Kyle asked.

Dave looked to see if Alex, Owen, or Erica were coming back, but there was no sign of them. "Alex told me that you like Erica. He said so when we were walking through the old part of Woodbrook."

Kyle laughed. "I think it's him that likes her. I don't have any interest in her; she's just a friend. Her face cleared up, and I bet he isn't man enough to admit he likes her. He's a strange guy."

"I bet you're right," Lauren said. "I know he used to talk shit about her, but things changed when he saw her today."

Kyle thought back to earlier when Lauren and Erica had shown up at Dave's house. Alex had definitely gravitated to Erica.

"Well, let's just stop talking about them. They'll probably be back any minute now," Dave said.

"For sure," Lauren said.

Kyle noticed the box of beer on the ground that Owen had earlier. Kyle had completely forgotten about it. Dave opened a can and took a sip before offering it to Lauren. She shook her head.

"It's not my thing, Dave. I tried it before, and it tastes horrible."

"You're right," Dave said. "It does taste bad."

The rain started to come down harder on them.

"I hope they get back soon," Lauren said, her teeth chattering. "I'm going to be soaked by the time I get home. I wish I had Erica's red coat."

"Let's give them ten more minutes," Kyle said. "Here, let's shelter." They ran to a big tree, but Dave stayed by the oil drum. He rolled his eyes at them both sheltering under the tree.

"Good idea, Kyle."

"You know it!"

After taking another sip of the beer, Dave threw it into the drum. The can made a large clang, clearly still almost full.

"Beer wasn't so good, huh?" Kyle joked.

Dave ignored him and headed in the direction Erica and Owen had taken. Within a few seconds, he disappeared into the foliage.

"Do you think that something is bothering him?" Lauren asked Kyle.

"Maybe. He was fine just a minute ago. I hope he's okay. We don't need anyone else to be mad."

"Maybe the rain is affecting his mood," she said.

Kyle smiled and extended his hand out to catch the rain. "I don't mind it. The sound of it helps me sleep."

"For sure!"

About a minute later, the rain ceased. The two of them went back to the drum. The branches and the pieces of wood were now black and soggy.

"I don't want to go back to school on Monday," Kyle said.

"Ditto," she responded. "I've got a geometry test later this week. I've never been a fan of math."

"I enjoy it, but I can see how others wouldn't. They give you homework for it every day, and no one really likes that."

Lauren smiled. "I wish we had classes together. Well, besides the gym class that we had together last year."

Kyle felt the same way. He now saw a chance for him to ask her something. "Dave is having a house party in a few weeks. No adults. Do you want to join us?"

Lauren tried to smile. "I wish I could, but I can't. My parents don't want me going to a place without any parental supervision. They'd kill me if they found out that no parents were around."

"What about in the tree house?" Kyle asked. "The six of us were up there alone."

"Our parents were at Dave's house while we were up there. I looked out of the treehouse window at least twice, and one of those times, my mother was looking over at us from a window."

"I understand that you can't go then, Lauren. It would've been nice if you were there, but maybe another time."

"Of course, I'll be able to see you around school until then."

Kyle started to inch closer to Lauren. He wanted to see how she reacted. She didn't move away as he got closer.

"Does your mom know that you're with us now?"

She shook her head. "She thinks that I'm just with Erica. I told her we were going to a movie."

"Won't she expect you home soon?"

"I told her that we might go to the mall. Erica's older brother Chris would drive us if we needed to get around. We never even asked her brother if he would, but I needed some reason to be out here for a few hours."

"That's lit, Lauren."

"My mother is very paranoid. I guess she should be sometimes. I never told her this, but I was around a few people a few months back that were drunk. They had a car they wanted to drive. I refused and walked home. The girl that wanted to drive was sixteen, so she just got her license. I won't mention her name, but she treated me differently in school after that. I don't associate with her at all now."

Kyle thought about who that girl might be. No one came to mind, so he decided to drop the thought. It really didn't matter anyways.

"What about your father?' Kyle asked.

"What about him? Are you asking on what he thinks of my actions?"

Kyle nodded.

"I barely see him, Kyle. My parents aren't divorced, though. They are separated."

The sound of leaves crunching and branches snapping suddenly came from the area that the others went through earlier. Both of them looked over, and the sound stopped. Kyle thought someone might be spying on them, so he put his index finger over his mouth to Lauren. They stayed silent for about a minute until they heard Dave's voice.

"I think we should go home now; we found Alex."

Kyle approached the area where Dave's voice came from. "Is he with you now?"

Dave appeared out of the foliage. Kyle waited to see if someone else would come out, but nothing happened.

"We found him. I caught up with them. They told me to come back here and tell the two of you. They'll be back here in a few minutes."

"Is everything okay?" Lauren asked.

Dave looked at the ground and back up at Lauren. "Just wait until he gets back."

The Last Time

"Why can't you just tell us now, Dave?" Kyle asked.

Dave rolled his eyes. "Alex said he was going to go home by himself. Owen convinced him to come back with us. It didn't help that Erica was with us, but she said she was sorry for what she'd said to him earlier, so he agreed to walk back with us."

Lauren leaned over and whispered in Kyle's ear. "She didn't need to apologize. Alex was the one in the wrong."

Kyle nodded his head.

The sound of voices came from the foliage. Almost right away, Kyle recognized Owen's.

"Let's do this again, Alex. Maybe you can hang with me, Trent, and Glen here. It will be different than today."

Kyle presumed that Owen wanted to go with Alex and Erica along with some of his other friends to Dade Woods. It sounded as if would not include Kyle and Lauren. Kyle didn't like being excluded, but maybe it was something that Alex needed.

Erica appeared first, with Alex right behind her. He had a cigarette in his mouth and a tiny bottle of gin in his left hand. Owen followed them.

"Everything alright now?" Kyle asked.

"I'm done buggin'," Alex replied.

"Shall we go home now?" Lauren asked, looking at Owen.

Owen opened up a beer. It sprayed all over his hands. "Fuckin' beer!"

"Good one, dude," Dave said sarcastically.

"No, I want to stay around here for a bit," Owen replied. "I think we should enjoy our freedom. Back to school tomorrow."

Kyle wondered why Alex didn't laugh about the beer spraying. Usually, he would have. It was as if he had lost his sense of humor while he'd gone off. Instead of looking at anyone, he stared at the oil drum and dragged on his cigarette.

"I was thinking of having a party at my house in a few weeks," said Dave. "My parents will be gone. They trust me with the house."

"I'll be there," Owen said.

"Me too," Erica added.

"Count me in," Alex said.

"I don't think I can make it," Lauren responded, looking away.

Owen finished his beer and threw it into the oil drum. "Why not?"

Before Lauren could say anything, Kyle asked, "What day is it?"

"It'll be three weeks from yesterday. That's December 16th," Dave replied.

Kyle didn't want to go if Lauren wasn't. He had to think of an excuse quickly. "I'm at my cousin's that weekend. We always see them a week or so before Christmas."

"I've similar plans," Lauren said. "My parents make us go to Green Bay to see my grandparents."

"It would've been fun with you two," Dave said. "We could've all met as the FTC for a few minutes beforehand."

Kyle liked that idea, but he knew there was no way they'd his cousin story if he changed his mind now. Instead, he just nodded and kept silent.

"Sorry, we can do the FTC another time," Lauren proposed. "Maybe in January?"

"Hella good idea," Dave said. "That way, it'll just be the six of us."

"I think it's time for us to go home," Erica said.

"Already?" Owen asked.

Erica tapped her foot against the oil drum. "I didn't tell my parents that Lauren and I were going with you guys. They're expecting me home in about an hour. I told them my brother Chris would be driving us around. He agreed to say he was, and I want to make sure I get home before he does."

"Let's bounce," Alex said.

"I want to stay here and have another beer and a few cigs," Owen said.

"I'll stay here too," Dave added.

"Alex? Kyle? Are you going to stay with us or leave with them?" Owen asked, pointing at the two girls.

"I'll stay here with you boys," Alex replied. "I want another gin bottle if you still have any left."

Kyle shifted uncomfortably. "I think I'll go with the girls. I've got a major test on Tuesday, so I'd better start studying."

Owen glared at Kyle.

"Okay, the three of you go. I'll see you at school tomorrow," Owen said.

"Kyle, I'll see you in gym class," Dave said. "Hopefully we don't have a fitness test."

"Remember that no one needs to know about what we did here," said Owen. "I don't want any of my coaches hearing about my cigs or the booze."

"No problem," Kyle said.

"We're going to take a different way home," said Erica. "I don't want to be seen by my parents."

"Good idea," Owen said.

Erica walked away without saying goodbye. Lauren and Kyle waved to the others.

As they left the trees, they could see clear sky ahead of them, though it was still cold. The weather didn't matter to Kyle. He was just glad to be with Lauren. Hopefully, they could have a good conversation despite Erica being with them.

As teenagers, it was the last time they were all together. Despite it being a short amount of time, the comradery they felt as the FTC would stay with them forever.

Going Home

Kyle, Lauren and Erica left Dade Woods in a hurry so that the girls wouldn't get in trouble with their parents. They decided to take a different way home, skipping the cemetery and the lifeless downtown. Instead, they traveled via some streets with less traffic. It was only about a half-mile difference and would take five to ten more minutes. An underpass went under Madsen Boulevard, so they headed that way.

"I enjoyed our walk today," Lauren said to Kyle. "I think all of us should do it again."

"Yes, it was good despite how Alex acted," Erica said.

Kyle asked, "So what happened when you went to look for Alex?"

"Let's keep going. I'll tell you as soon as we get to that tunnel."

Lauren said, "I hope you have fun at Dave's house in a couple of weeks."

"Your mom won't let you go, right?" Erica asked Lauren.

"You're correct. I want to go, but I don't have a good enough lie. She'd probably check up on me no matter what I told her."

"What about today? Are you afraid of her finding out you were with us?" Kyle asked.

Lauren shrugged her shoulders. "Erica's brother Chris will vouch for us, so I'm not worried about that. A party with no adults is a different thing."

"How's it different?" Erica asked.

"Because I know there'll be alcohol and probably worse there. There'll also be cigarettes. She'd smell the alcohol on my breath and the smoke on my clothes."

"It's always good to be safe," Kyle commented.

"You need to take some risks in your life," Erica said.

"Maybe another day, Erica."

"How about you, Kyle? Are you lying like Lauren?"

Kyle scratched the back of his head. "No, I do have to see my relatives. I'm not lying." He felt uncomfortable lying, but he still didn't want to be there if Lauren wasn't.

Erica said, "It'll be a good time. Your mom needs to chillax."

"Sorry if I sound like a buzzkill, Erica. My family are just protective. My cousin Heather was caught drinking at a party when she was sixteen. She was grounded for about six months."

"Okay, Lauren. I won't say anything more about it," Erica said.

They now approached the tunnel underneath Madsen Boulevard. The sidewalk gradually dipped until it curved into the entrance of the pedestrian tunnel.

It was about seven feet high with graffiti on the walls, but Kyle couldn't make out what it said.

"Okay, tell us about when you found Alex," said Kyle to Erica. "Sorry, but I really want to know."

"Well, we didn't find him," Erica said. "He found us."

"Tell me more," Kyle said.

"He had a sad look on his face. Owen asked him to hang out with some of his friends another time as maybe it would make Alex feel better. It sounded like it would be just them and not any of us. Owen felt bad for him and so did I. I know he talked a lot of shit about me, but I couldn't help it. I told him I was sorry about how I acted earlier. I know it sounds stupid, but I just didn't want any more conflict. Alex had this hollow look that I can't really describe. It made me worried about him. I know he likes to joke a lot, but in reality, he's a pretty chill guy. I think he hides behind his humor. At least, that's what I think. I'm trying to understand him, so I need to tolerate his antics. My mother has warned me about guys like him. It's just best to humor him and then leave it be."

Kyle now had an idea about how Erica really felt about Alex. "Do you like him?"

Erica smiled. "He wishes I liked him. If he likes me, he has a bad way of showing it."

Kyle knew that she was avoiding the question, so he decided to drop it.

"Either way, I'm glad that you and Alex have at least patched things up," Lauren said. "He doesn't seem to be in a good place right now."

"I don't even want to talk about him anymore!" Erica said.

"Let's get out of this tunnel," Lauren said.

The tunnel was only about forty feet long. Daylight streamed in at the end of the tunnel, but it wasn't lit on this grey day, so the middle was quite dark. Kyle thought about all the horror stories he had read about monsters in dark places like this.

"Why are you walking so slow?" Lauren asked him.

"I just want to make sure I don't step in a puddle or anything gnarly. It's hard to see here."

"Gnarly! That's a word I haven't heard in a while," said Erica. "I think I'll start using it again."

"You do that," he responded.

They made it to the end of the tunnel about a minute later. Lauren sped up.

"In a hurry, Lauren?" Kyle asked.

"I just want to see if any cars are driving by here? Let me do this by myself. I know what I'm looking out for."

Kyle and Erica waited at the end of the tunnel while Lauren scouted out the street above.

Kyle said, "Do you think she's being paranoid?"

"She just wants to make sure her mother isn't there."

"Is her mother *that* strict?"

Erica rolled her eyes. "Yes, she is. It makes Lauren question everything she does. Her mother had Lauren without being married. That was a big no-no for the grandparents. Lauren's mother doesn't want that to happen to Lauren."

"Okay, I understand now. It seems as if her mother thinks that Lauren could have the same situation. I don't think that would happen to Lauren, but parents sometimes only see it through their own experiences."

The two of them stood in silence as they waited for Lauren to come back. About a minute later, they heard footsteps coming down the sidewalk.

"I saw my neighbor's car on the road. Of all the times they had to be out there! I don't know if they saw me."

"You've got to be shittin' me!" Erica said.

"What now?" Kyle asked.

Lauren sat down and leaned against the wall of the tunnel. "I guess wait a few minutes, then try again."

Erica sat next to her. "Maybe just Lauren and I should leave the tunnel. Kyle, you can go out maybe five or ten minutes after. Lauren doesn't need to get caught hanging out with a boy."

Before Kyle could say anything, Lauren looked him in the eye. "That may be for the best."

"I'm okay with it," Kyle said.

Erica and Lauren got up and walked away. Before they were out of sight, Lauren turned and waved goodbye. Kyle waved back, and she gave him a big smile.

After she was out of sight, Kyle said, "I hope to see you again soon."

Back in the House

Things were never the same after that day. Kyle saw Lauren around school, but he couldn't hang out with her. They didn't have any classes together once the new semester started. He tried to call her once, but her mother answered the phone, so he hung up. He never got the nerve to call again. Alex got in more trouble at school and kept his distance from the other five. Dave, Owen, and Kyle went as a group to prom, but after that, they were never together again. Lauren went to prom with Brent Fargo, but Kyle didn't speak to her. Erica and Kyle bumped into each other around town a couple of times, but they never hung out. After high school, they all went their separate ways.

They could've hung out in the treehouse again, but they never did as a group of six. At that age, Kyle thought there would be more times for it to happen. He now knew that nothing lasted forever, and many times, you never know when doing something will be the last time you ever do it.

After reminiscing about that November day, Kyle suddenly realized that it was getting late, and Lauren might now be asleep. He stepped off the porch, entered the house, and listened. Voices came from the den. When he wandered in, and saw that the came from the TV, but there was no one was watching it. A drink was on the table next to the couch. He picked up the glass and smelled it; it was gin.

As Kyle went past the kitchen and down the hall, he saw that the light in the bathroom was still on. He knocked gingerly on the door. After no reply, he quickly peeked inside, but it was empty. At the end of the hall, in the dimness, he saw Lauren on the bottom bunk in the room on the left. Her suitcase was open, and clothes were all over the floor. Her blue jeans had been flung over the arm of the small loveseat in there. He waited to see if she'd say anything, but she didn't.

Edging closer, he could see her face clearly from the little bit of light from the hallway that shined into the room. Her mouth was open, and her eyes were closed. His heart raced as he looked at her.

"Sweet dreams," he whispered.

He closed the door to her room; now he needed a room for himself. After looking at the room across the hall, he saw it had a king-sized bed. He often moved around a lot in his sleep, so it would be perfect for him.

After entering the room, he realized that his luggage was still in the car, so he went back outside to get it. There was a full moon, which made him wish Lauren was awake so they could see it together. He always liked seeing a full moon. It was hard to take his eyes away from it.

After taking his luggage out of the back seat, he received a text.

ALEX: Sorry that I haven't responded in the last few hours.

KYLE: Where are you?

ALEX: I made it on the train and got off but

KYLE: But what?

ALEX: I needed some time to myself

KYLE: You could've told someone!

ALEX: I should have

KYLE: Where are you now?

ALEX: I'm at the Dryden Motel

KYLE: Near the train station?

ALEX: Yep

KYLE: Overnight?

ALEX: Yes. I'll come by tomorrow

KYLE: Will you need someone to pick you up?

ALEX: I'll walk over

KYLE: You sure?

Alex didn't respond right away. Kyle leaned against his car for a few minutes, waiting for Alex to text back. After about five minutes and no reply, Kyle decided to walk back to the house.

"I hope you show up tomorrow, Alex," Kyle said to himself.

As Kyle was about to enter the house via the side door, he saw the treehouse. He wondered what it looked like inside now. Back when they were teenagers, there was a Nirvana poster in there, along with a radio that had CD and cassette players. Dave used to play many songs in there, but the ones that stuck out to Kyle were *Enter Sandman* by Metallica and *Can't Help Falling in Love* by UB40. The latter one seemed to play on the radio all the time during the summer of 1993.

Despite the urge to go into the treehouse, Kyle decided it would be best to wait for all five of them to go in together. He hoped that'd be tomorrow.

Once Kyle got back to the bedroom, he unloaded his clothes and put them in the empty chest of drawers. At first, it felt weird that his clothes were going into the drawers that used to belong to Dave's parents. He'd never been into their room until today. Their door had always been closed whenever Kyle had gone around.

Before going to bed, he peeked behind the other bedroom door and took one last look at Lauren. She was still in the same position on the bottom bunk. He hoped that his sleep would be just as peaceful.

Late Night

A faint buzzing sound woke Kyle up in the king-sized bed a few hours later. He checked his phone. There was a new text.

ALEX: I'll walk over in the morning

Kyle noticed that it was now 2 a.m., over two hours since Alex had last texted.

KYLE: What took you so long? I waited for your answer!
ALEX: Sorry. I was at Rafferty's bar trying to pick up some girl
KYLE: Are you with her now?
ALEX: No. That twat wasn't interested
KYLE: Do you want me to pick you up?
ALEX: No
KYLE: You sure?
ALEX: YES. I told you I'd be there in the morning
KYLE: OK
ALEX: Is Lauren there with you?
KYLE: Yes

ALEX: In the bed with you?

KYLE: No

ALEX: Why not?

KYLE: Do you have anything more that you need right now? I want to go back to sleep

ALEX: Nothing now

KYLE: I'll see you in the mornin

ALEX: I'll be there before 10 am

KYLE: OK, be safe

    Kyle could barely keep his eyes open. However, he had to pee, so he got up and went to the bathroom. After finishing his leak, he wandered into the dark hallway. Looking at the bunk bed, he stopped. Lauren was no longer in there. Looking back into his room, he saw her standing by his bed, her arms crossed. She was wearing grey workout shorts and a black tank top. He had never seen her so scantily clad before.

    "Trouble sleeping, Lauren?"

    "I heard you leave your room, so I got up. Now I'm wide awake."

    Kyle pointed at his phone. "Alex texted me. He's in town. He'll stop by here in the morning."

    "I hope he keeps up with his part of the bargain. Hopefully he'll leave soon after. I bet he'll be just as much of a pain as he was when we were teens. Him going AWOL earlier really pissed me off."

"That reminds me," Kyle said.

"Of what?" she asked, yawning.

"Back when we took that walk to Dade Woods in the mid-nineties, I wondered how Erica and Owen got Alex to come back with them. Erica said she felt bad for him, but I feel there was more to it."

Lauren sat on the front of the bed. "Yes, there was more to it. Erica told me about it a few months later."

"What happened?"

Yawning again, Lauren lay back on the bed. "From what I was told, Owen promised Alex some drugs if he came back with them. Glen and Trent would join them."

"Interesting," Kyle said. "I guess I had good intuition back then."

"There's more, Kyle,"

"Okay, tell me."

Lauren sat back up. "I remember that you asked her if Erica liked Alex. She denied it, but it was true. She also liked Owen, but she felt he was way out of her league, so I guess Alex was a better fit in her mind."

"I was right again," Kyle said.

"Yes, you were. She and Alex had a relationship of sorts later. I believe it was for a short period in high school. I never really got any specifics on that. He made her mad a few months into it, so it ended. I think he started talking shit about her again."

Kyle sighed. "I guess there might be some friction between them once they're back both back here. What a joy that'll be!"

Lauren laughed. "I love your sarcasm! I think you're right, Kyle."

After some hesitation, Kyle sat on the bed near Lauren. He wanted to see if she'd move away, but she didn't. Instead, she placed her hand in his. He gave it a squeeze.

"I hope that I can tell you soon about my issue. I want to say it the right way," Lauren said.

"Now is as good a time as any," Kyle said.

Lauren shrugged her shoulders. "I think I need a little bit more time."

"Understood," Kyle said, kissing her on the temple.

"Where have you been all my life?" she asked.

"I could say the same thing about you, Lauren. I wish that we hadn't lost touch."

After attempting to smile, Lauren looked away and stared at the wall. "My twenties were a difficult time for me."

Kyle wanted to ask her what she meant, but figured asking her about it might make her leave the room. Instead, he inched closer to her on the bed. She had a scent of the most appealing perfume he had ever smelled.

"I'm glad we're alone. Even though Alex is unreliable, he actually did us a favor by not being here," Kyle said.

Lauren rested her head on his shoulder. "You're right. I do hope he's pleasant to be around, though."

"Same. I'm not even sure how pleasant Owen and Erica will be. Owen seemed very cocky when I was on the phone with him."

"What about him was cocky?" Lauren asked.

"He's doing very well with his house-building business. He bragged about being smart enough to soak up the knowledge of running a business. I'm not sure if that kind of cockiness will mesh well with Alex."

"Aren't you doing well as a lawyer, too?"

Kyle turned a slight shade of red. "I've had a few good cases that got me a decent payday. I won't brag about it, though. I have some money saved, but it won't last for the rest of my life."

"Do you like being a lawyer?" she asked, taking her head off his shoulder.

He shook his head. "To tell the truth, I don't particularly. I've been thinking of getting out of the profession. Like I said, I'm doing well, but I only want that so I can do something else and buy somewhere decent. Maybe a house in a small town. At least a suburb that's not too big. Living in a big city has never been my ideal place. I'm only there as it's easy to drive to my firm. I could possibly open my own business. I've always liked to collect stuff. I've got a ton of baseball and football cards. I also have some autographed baseballs. I could maybe open collectables shop in a small town. I don't own a fancy car, and I live a modest life.

I like to have nice things, but I don't need to show it off to everyone. I feel that if someone shows off for approval, it's other people's opinions that rule their life."

"True that," she said, lying on her back again.

"I think that over the next few days, I'll decide what I'm going to do. Maybe I need to make a change from law sooner rather than later. I don't want to rush the decision, though. Some time away should help. If I do move somewhere, I want it to be something I won't regret, Lauren."

There was no response from her. He looked over; she was out cold. Her legs hung over the edge of the bed, so he started moving her onto the bed. She woke up for a second and murmured something unintelligible.

After she was in a good position to sleep, he went back to the TV room by the front door. His mind was racing about the thought of possibly moving out of Cincinnati. It would be a big step that couldn't be decided on a whim. That thought would make him toss and turn, and he didn't want to bother Lauren by doing that.

    The TV was still on, so he sat on the couch and tried to find something to watch. There was a channel that just played classical music. Perfect! The soft sounds of the channel soothed him until he fell asleep on the sofa a few minutes later.

Early Morning

"Kyle, it's time to wake up," Lauren said.

He opened his eyes and saw her standing in front of the TV. She was wearing a white bathrobe, and her hair was wet. He fought to stop his eyes from closing again. At first, it felt like a dream, but he knew it wasn't. His first thought was whether she was wearing anything underneath that robe.

"Sorry to wake you," she said. "Alex has just arrived and is upstairs picking a room."

"Is it 10 am already?"

"No,' she replied. "It's 8:35 am. He showed up about fifteen minutes ago. He knocked on my window and woke me up."

"That's so typical of him, Lauren. He told me that he'd be here around ten. I set my phone to wake me at nine."

"Yeah, I wonder if he was staring at me in the bunk. After I let him in, I took a quick shower."

Lauren left the room, and Kyle stood up. He was still in his clothes from the night before, so he decided to take a quick shower. After the shower, he put on a bath robe and headed towards his room. Lauren was now fully dressed in blue denim shorts with the pockets sticking out bottom and a tucked-in grey t-shirt. Behind the clingy fabric, he could tell that her stomach was flat and toned.

"I'll be ready in a few minutes; not sure what we're going to do until the others get here," Kyle said.

"Hopefully they'll be here soon," she said, pointing upstairs to where Alex probably still was. She left the room a few seconds later.

Kyle put on his tan cargo shorts and a new collared blue polo shirt. After taking a quick look in the bedroom mirror, he went to the kitchen. Lauren was sitting at the table. The kitchen window was open, allowing a fresh breeze to waft around the room.

"Do you want to go out to eat this morning, Kyle?"

"Sure. Let's see if Alex wants to come with us. If not, just you and me, babe."

Some banging came from the stairs, and Alex cried out.

"He's fallen!" Kyle cried. Getting up, Kyle quickly shot to the stairs. "Alex, are you okay?"

He found Alex stood on the stairs, a smirk on his face. His unshaven face, sly smile, and slicked-back hair made him look mean; it wasn't how Kyle would've pictured him. He had blue jeans on and a navy T-shirt that said *Za's Vid!* in white letters. The shirt didn't hide his slight paunch.

"You frightened the shit out of me, Alex! I thought you'd fallen down the stairs," Kyle said.

"Nope, I wanted to fool the two of you."

"I thought you were done with joking around," Kyle said. "You said so on the phone yesterday."

"I guess good habits die hard, Kyle."

"Okay, I guess they sometimes do."

Alex came down the stairs as Kyle's phone buzzed with a new text.

ERICA: I've arrived. Got an earlier flight. I'm getting a rental car now. Be there around noon.
KYLE: Great! See you then
ERICA: Who's there now?
KYLE: Lauren and Alex
ERICA: Lovely ☹
KYLE: What do you mean by that?

Kyle figured her response was about Alex, but he wanted to be sure. He wanted another minute to see if she'd respond, but none came.

"Erica will be here around noon-ish. We're just waiting on Owen after that."

"I got a text from Owen this morning," Alex said. "He'll probably be here around noon too."

Finally, the five of them would be together.

"We can all go out for dinner," Kyle said. "As for now, shall we go for lunch in a few hours?"

"I'm okay, Kyle-Pile. I'm not hungry now and probably won't be then. If you and Lauren want to go somewhere together, I can stay here and maybe take a nap. It's up to you."

Alex was still calling people by nicknames. If he started to call Owen 'Sewer' instead of Seward, there might be a scuffle. Kyle hoped that wouldn't happen.

Alex continued, "I found a room upstairs that isn't being used. It's the one closest to Dave's room. I put my stuff in there already. I didn't sleep much last night."

"Where did you spend the night?"

"I passed out by the side of the bar around 4:30, I think."

"You haven't changed, Alex," Kyle commented.

"It's my life, Kyle."

Kyle didn't want to say anything about how reckless Alex had been or Alex would accuse him of being judgmental. Thankfully, Alex went back upstairs.

Kyle pulled up a seat and sat next to Lauren. "I don't know if I want to leave him alone in this house. I know it sounds weird, but I've got a bad feeling. His behavior last night tells me how reckless he can be. Let's skip going out for breakfast today."

"I was thinking the same thing. That's why I was hiding in here. He's gives me the creeps. Maybe I can make something here from the food in the cabinets."

"Good luck, Lauren."

She opened the freezer and found a full loaf of bread inside. Kyle didn't even think of looking in there earlier. After taking out the bread, she grabbed two cans of tuna from a cupboard and put them on the counter.

"Tuna on white bread, okay?" she asked. "The bread will need to thaw for a little bit, though."

"Sounds good. I didn't even notice that when I got here."

"Don't have any mayo, though."

"All good."

Lauren began preparing their breakfast once the bread had defrosted. Kyle hadn't had that kind of sandwich in probably a decade. His mother used to make him tuna sandwiches with mayo, lettuce, and tomato. He always had it with a Dr. Pepper or Coke.

After getting two glasses of water out of a Brita pitcher, Lauren came back to the table with the food.

Kyle leaned over and put his mouth close to her ear. "I was surprised at how Alex looked. He's sort of mean-looking to me."

"I think he's still joking around. I don't know what to make of him yet."

The sandwich wasn't delectable, but it would do for the moment. The absence of mayo and salad made a huge difference. After eating half the sandwich, Kyle looked at his phone to see another text.

ERICA: I mean that I'm not looking forward to seeing Alex. I know I need to, but I don't want to
KYLE: Please be civil
ERICA: Stuff has happened since we were teens. I can tell you about it another time
KYLE: OK. See you in a bit
ERICA: See ya

Kyle showed Lauren Erica's texts. She shook her head.

"Guess we'll get the full story," Kyle said.

Kyle finished his sandwich and washed it down with the water. "The funny thing is that when I called him yesterday, he said that he'd got in trouble in college, which had taught him a lesson. I wonder if that was a lie or if his bad habits have started up again because he's meeting us, like some sort of regression."

"I'm not a shrink, so I'm not sure. I just hope that he doesn't piss off Owen at all. I remember Alex used to make fun of Owen's last name."

Kyle put his plate and glass in the sink. "I was thinking the same thing. Owen had a temper in high school, and Alex liked to provoke people."

"On another note," Kyle said, grabbing Lauren's plate and glass, "that walk was a fun day, except for Alex's name-calling. It was the first time I really got to know you."

"I wish there had been more days like that, Kyle. We didn't have another day like that during high school. My mother got in the way of me spending time with many of my friends outside of school, especially in my later years of high school. I was lucky that I even got to go to some school functions."

Kyle sat back down at the table. "That day has never left me. I've thought of it many times. In fact, I thought about it last night. It's all very vivid to me still."

Lauren reached her hand out and put it in his. "If I could go back to one day in my life, that'd probably be it. It was a simple day but so memorable. I'm sad to say that there haven't been many great days in my life."

Kyle was about to lean over and kiss her when another text interrupted.

OWEN: I'm at the airport and will be leaving soon. I'll be landing at 11:52 a.m.

KYLE: Thanks. Erica landed a few minutes ago and will be here by noon.

OWEN: I'll be there a little bit after that.

KYLE: Talk again soon

While Kyle was texting, Lauren headed to the living room. He followed her and found her looking at the framed photo that Kyle had spotted the night before, the one of him and Dave as kids.

"We really can't go back, can we?" she asked.

"Do you mean back in time when we were young?"

Lauren nodded.

"I guess all we can do is learn from our past," Kyle said. "I'd love to go back and experience some of my early childhood, but with the mind I had back then and not the one I have now."

"Are you in this picture?" she asked, holding it out to Kyle.

"I am." He pointed to himself in the photo. "The others are Alex, Dave, and a kid named Felix. I'm not sure what even happened to him."

Lauren's eyes went wide. "Do you mean Felix Monahan?"

Kyle had to think a moment about whether that was his last name, then nodded.

"He lived a few blocks from me but went to another junior high," said Lauren. "I heard that he transferred to some private school at the end of his freshmen year. Not the one that Erica went to, though. He was always the nicest guy. His mom raised him, and she worked three jobs so he could go to that private school."

"Interesting. I don't remember much about him. He was Dave's friend. I didn't hang out with him much."

"I completely forgot about him. I'll have to see if he's on Facebook sometime. He's probably successful now. He was an underdog."

After taking another glimpse of the photo, Lauren bit her lip, and her eyes became glassy. "I still need to come to grips with the fact that Dave is gone. I know I lost contact with him, but it seems so unreal that he's gone."

Kyle sat down on the couch and patted the cushion next to him. Lauren put the picture back on the bookcase and sat next to him. Her legs looked so smooth that he couldn't help staring at them for a few seconds. He realized that she might notice him staring, so he looked away.

"I've got a question for you, Kyle."

"Go ahead."

"What're your plans? Are you going to leave here once everyone else does?"

Kyle wasn't sure where this conversation was going. He hoped she was leading up to asking if they could spend some time together.

"One of Dave's relatives said this house will be given to someone within ten days. I have no idea who it is. Probably someone that I don't even know. I may stay here until then. I'm not really sure."

"Okay, would you mind if I come visit you in Cincinnati in maybe two or three weeks from now?"

"I'd like that," Kyle said. "Is everything okay?"

She looked down at the carpet. "I just thought about something that used to happen to me as a teenager."

"Is this what your secret is about?"

She sighed. "No, it isn't that. This couch we're on just reminded me of some of my teenage times."

Kyle tried not to look confused but couldn't help it. "How does this couch remind you of that?"

"My mother had the same model of couch in blue instead of red. I used to spend a good amount of time on it," she said, gripping one of the cushions.

"Is it a bad memory?"

She softened her grip on the cushion.

"You know that my mother was strict. In high school, I wasn't allowed to do much with friends. She grew up around here and went to Pine School, the one that most kids thought was haunted. My mother would often make me stay at home. I'd sit on the couch, look out the window, and wonder what my friends were doing. I felt so lonely. I had to beg her to let me go to Homecoming that one time you went with Holly Gianetti. The same for when I went to Senior Prom."

"I'm sorry, Lauren."

"Do you remember that time when Dave asked us to go to a party at his house, and I said I couldn't because I was going to Green Bay?" Lauren asked. "This was while we were in Dade Woods."

Kyle had to think, but he remembered. It was when he didn't want to go as Lauren was not going.

"Yes, I remember."

"That was a lie, Kyle. I had to make that up as I knew my mother wouldn't let me go. I was so embarrassed to say that to everyone."

"I'm sorry that happened. I knew she was strict, but not to that degree."

Lauren stood up and went over to the piano, grazing her fingers over its varnished frame. "I remember one time the Fourth of July parade went by. It had to be the summer between my junior and senior years. I was made to stay home that day. I saw the parade pass from the window. You were in it, and so were Owen and Dave."

"Yes, we were doing charity work for the YMCA," Kyle said. "My parents thought it would look good for my college application. We had a canned food drive."

"That must've been it. I only brought this up because I started to get the same feeling that I did that day. It echoed within me. Luckily, I'm not in that situation now. I felt that the parade was like my life passing me by. You didn't even know I wanted to come and see you."

"Your mother wouldn't even let you go outside that day?"

She turned around and looked at Kyle. "I guess it was extreme at that time. Some other times she was normal. I felt like a prisoner sometimes."

"Well," Kyle said. "You're not a prisoner right now, so don't dwell on it. I understand it was a bad time, but we're here now, and you're free."

Kyle was afraid that what he'd said may have sounded too harsh. After a few seconds of tense silence, he held out his hand.

"Are you going to be alright?" he asked.

"Yes, I think I'll be."

Two tears ran down her cheeks. She smiled, wiped her tears away, and put her hand in his. To Kyle's delight, she sat on his lap.

"No one has ever made me feel the way you have in these past twelve hours. I don't want this time to end, Kyle."

Kyle felt that the moment was perfect. He didn't want to say anything more as it might make it less perfect. Words couldn't describe how he felt now. Even the most poetic words would do nothing to convey his feelings. Instead, he put his head on her shoulder. All he wanted to do was be with her in comfortable silence.

Sudden Arrival

"Wakey, wakey, Kyle. Time to get up." Alex yelled.

Kyle and Lauren jumped, bumping heads.

"You dumb shit! You could've announced yourself more gently," Lauren snapped.

Lauren quickly got off Kyle's lap and left. Alex's eyes followed her, but he didn't say anything.

"Good one, dipshit," Kyle said. "Couldn't you see we were having a moment?"

Alex clenched his teeth and crossed his arms. "Don't make a big deal out of it. It's not like you won't be able to bang her later tonight or anything."

Kyle grabbed the arm of the couch tightly. "Don't say stuff like that. You don't even know what's going on between her and me. Keep your remarks to yourself and think before you speak."

"What's up your ass?"

Kyle's heartbeat quickened. He felt this conversation wasn't going to get any better. Alex stared at him straight.

"You know what, Alex? I was hoping you were more mature now. You told me on the phone yesterday that you'd got yourself together because of something that happened in college, but it's like you've regressed to being a teenager again as soon as you got back in town."

Alex uncrossed his arms and looked away. "Well, I forgot that you were a killjoy and could never have a bit of fun. Not everything is serious. I guess I'll tone it down if both of you are so touchy about everything."

"Okay, I hope that you will. It's great that you're here. You kept your part of the promise, and I'm glad you did. It was what Dave wanted," Kyle said.

"I'm glad to be here, Kyle. For Dave."

"Okay, I'm sorry about how I spoke to you."

Alex crossed his arms again. "Yeah, well, it happens."

There was no apology from Alex as Kyle had hoped. Instead, Alex looked around the room, then left.

Kyle went to find Lauren. She wasn't on either of the bunks, or in his room. Since Alex had claimed a room upstairs, it was doubtful she'd gone up there. The only other options were the basement or outside. Kyle chose the former to check first.

Kyle found the light on when he went down the basement stairs. He looked around the large room. The floor was now bamboo. When he'd been down there as a kid, it had been a lime green Pergo flooring. Despite the bamboo looking great, he missed the way it had been. The Pergo had a smooth feeling and was often cold in the winter.

The basement was mostly empty except for a green couch with holes in it, and the old stereo system that Dave used to play CDs on when they were teens.

"I'm over here, Kyle."

Kyle turned and saw Lauren in the back corner near a picture on the wall. It was the one that had freaked him out as a preteen. The picture was of a dining room table that wasn't being used, despite there being plates, silverware, and candles placed on it. It was supposedly haunted, as the candles on it would sometimes be lit, and other times they weren't. Kyle later found out that it was a trick picture because the candles would only be lit if there was a certain amount of sunlight on the picture.

"Do you remember this picture?" Lauren asked, pointing at it.

"I do. It was supposedly haunted. Are the candles lit or unlit?"

"Lit this time. I think I remember them being unlit," Lauren said.

Kyle couldn't help but laugh. "The things we believed as kids. Dave often tried to scare us with that picture. It's just one of those trick pictures. I saw the exact same picture on Amazon once. It's mass-produced."

Lauren straightened the crooked picture. "I miss those times. Everything was so much easier back then."

Kyle had said the same thing to his mother a few years back. His mother told him that she felt the same way about her younger years, and that her mother had said the same thing to her. It seemed to be something that almost every person felt at some point in their life.

"I'm sorry that Alex was acting like a dick. I had a conversation with him, and it seems he hasn't changed. I guess we have to put up with him for the next day or so."

"Well, it's not me that has to worry about him," she said. "I feel bad for Erica if he treats her that way.

"Speaking of which," Kyle said, looking at his watch, "she'll be here in a couple of hours. So will Owen."

"What time is it, Kyle?"

"Almost 10 o'clock."

Lauren walked over to the stereo. She pressed the power button, but no light appeared. Seeing it was unplugged, she plugged it in. The power light glowed amber.

There was a rack of CDs next to it. Kyle looked to see what music there was. Guns N' Roses, Nirvana, Primus, Dave Matthews Band, The Police, and Madonna were just a few of the artists. He couldn't see the CD that Lauren picked, so he leaned over.

"Which one is that?"

She held out the CD. "Do you remember *Fade Into You* by Mazzy Star?"

"Yes, I do. Dave played it down here when we were in high school. It was me, him, Owen and two other girls."

"Do you remember their names?"

Kyle didn't at first. Then he remembered one of them. "One of them was Lisa Marshall. I can't remember the other one. She didn't go to our school."

Lauren bit her lower lip. "I remember her. I wasn't a fan. I think she liked Owen. Wasn't she friends with Holly Gianetti?"

"I think you're right. This was before I went with Holly to Homecoming. I think we were all down here at the beginning of our junior year."

"What were you doing down here? Maybe I don't want to know?" Lauren asked.

Kyle rolled his eyes. "No, I wasn't doing anything with either of the girls. I know that Owen wanted to do stuff with the other girl, but nothing happened. The other girl was a tease, though. She flirted with Owen and got him interested in her."

"You sure you don't remember her name?" Lauren asked.

"I can ask Owen when he gets here. All I remember is that she was from another town."

Lauren smiled and put in the CD. "What were you doing when this song played?"

Kyle pointed to the floor. "I was lying there. The room was smoky. Owen and Dave were smoking cigs."

Lauren pressed play, and the nostalgic tune washed over them. After putting the CD case back on the rack, she lay down on a multicolored rug. She motioned with her index finger for him to lay by her. He lay down and put his hand in hers.

After the song ended, it played again. He didn't think about getting up to change the CD, happy to listen to the song again with Lauren. To him, it felt as if they were in high school again. He didn't want to end.

Precious Time

Fade into You must've played at least ten times as they lay on the floor. Kyle didn't get sick of it; their hands interlocked the whole time. Then they heard footsteps on the stairs.

"The two of you're wearing this song thin!"

Kyle let go of Lauren's hand and stood up. "You could just let us be, Alex."

To Kyle's surprise, Alex simply turned away and went back upstairs. Kyle felt relieved.

"Another great appearance by Alex. It's only been a short time, but I'm starting to get a bad feeling about him," Lauren said.

Kyle offered his hand to help her up.

"I guess not all people can be as good as you," Lauren said as he helped her stand up.

Kyle didn't know if she was joking, but then she leaned in and hugged him.

"I'm not going to let him ruin my time with you or the others, Lauren. Hopefully, we can all meet in the treehouse again tonight, and he'll leave afterward. I know it sounds bad, but it's how I feel."

Lauren went over to the stereo. She took out the Mazzy Star CD and put in another one. "I hope you like this next song."

Kyle recognized it instantly: *November Rain* by Guns N' Roses. It had been one of his favorite songs in his teenage years, and he still enjoyed it.

"I like this song. It reminds me think of our long walk that one day. Alex kind of alluded to it when it started to rain. It sounded corny then, but now it has meaning."

"It's bittersweet to me, Kyle. That is, up until today. I wasn't sure if I would ever hang out with you again."

Kyle smiled and then looked at his watch. It was almost midday. "The other two will be here soon. I think we should go upstairs."

"Let's listen to the rest of the song first," Lauren said.

Kyle nodded and stood next to her by the stereo. They both closed their eyes and listened all the way through to the final chord. Before they went upstairs, Lauren turned off the stereo.

Kyle wanted to sit in the living room until the others arrived. Once upstairs, he looked around, but Alex was nowhere to be found. From his room, Kyle looked out the window and saw Alex standing next to the treehouse tree. A cigarette hung from his mouth, and he held a plastic lighter.

"Is he out there?" Lauren asked.

"He looks lonely. I don't want to go out there, though. He might start acting like a jerk again. I'm going to wait in the TV room."

Just as Kyle was about to leave, Lauren's phone rang.

"I need to take this. Meet you in the TV room in a few," she said before walking to her room.

Kyle sat on the leather couch in the TV room. As usual, there was nothing to watch on, so he selected a music channel. This time, it was one that just played folk music. It was boring, and he wished there was something more to do. After a while, he wondered if Lauren was still on the phone. After peeking down the hall towards her room, he saw that the door was still closed.

He went outside to the front porch. It was just after eleven p.m. The weather was perfect: sunny, low 80s, and a slight breeze. The Adirondack chair looked cozy, so he settled into it, waiting for Erica and Owen to arrive.

Minutes later, a black 725 BMW pulled up to the front of the house. Owen got out: he was over six feet tall, maybe two-hundred and seventy pounds, with brown hair combed over. He wore Ray-Ban sunglasses and an unbuttoned black designer suit.

"Kyle Brighton, I can tell that's you from here!"

As Owen walked to the porch, Kyle noticed Owen's stomach hung over his pants. The athlete that Kyle had expected was gone. At a closer look, Owen was probably over three-hundred pounds.

Kyle stood up and met him on the porch. They shook hands, and Owen took off his glasses. An inch-long scar ran along the side of his left eye.

"It's good to see you, Owen. It has been a long time."

"I think it's been about twelve or thirteen years," Owen said, smoothing his expensive suit. "I know it wasn't long after I graduated from college. It's been too long. A lot has changed for me.".

"Yes, as you told me on the phone. I guess you're pretty well off now." Kyle didn't want to mention that he wasn't doing that poorly himself. He felt that Owen would probably try to out-do him if he did.

"It seems that you're about an hour early, Owen."

"I got an earlier flight, Kyle. I got lucky."

"No problem, Owen."

"Is everyone else here?"

"All but Erica. I think she'll be here any moment now."

"Great!" Owen said. "I thought I'd stop by here first, then find a hotel later. There used to be this hotel that I always wanted to stay at. It was near Madsen Boulevard, but I can't remember the name."

"I think you're talking about the Midwesterner Inn. It was always a place that people used to go to have flings. At least that's what I heard."

"Yep, that's it! It wasn't a dive, though. It was rustic, but I heard it had a certain charm. I think it has six rooms."

"You didn't call them to see if there was a room free?" Kyle asked.

"Nah. Thought I'd just wing it. There'll be other places to go to if nothing is available. There are a few hotels near the airport."

Kyle pointed at the front door. "You can always stay here. Alex is staying upstairs, and Lauren and I each have our own rooms."

Owen looked at the house. Then he looked down the street at the rest of the block with a laugh.

"What's so funny, Owen?"

"Simon Park's house. I heard that he went into the Marines after getting into some trouble. He was in the second Iraq War. I hear he trains soldiers, nowadays. That little nerdy guy is now a certified badass."

"Yes," Kyle said. It's funny how people change over the years."

Kyle opened the door and beckoned Owen to follow him inside.

"One sec. I've got something for the gang."

Owen went back to his car and came back with a bottle of Dom Perignon. Kyle had never tried it before and was keen to.

As they arrived at the kitchen table, Lauren showed up, her phone in her hand, and her eyes wide as if she was surprised that Owen was there. Owen set the bottle on the table and opened his arms. He and Lauren embraced, then the three of them sat at the table.

"You look great, Lauren," Owen said.

"Thank you, Owen. I don't feel great considering what happened to Dave."

"Bittersweet, I guess." Owen responded.

"It is for all of us," Kyle said.

"Do you want to open this bottle now?" Owen asked, pointing to the champagne.

Lauren shook her head. "Let's wait until all five of us are here. Maybe tonight before we all go back to the treehouse."

"Sounds good," Owen said.

Lauren tapped her fingers against the table. "Alex is outside. I'm not sure if you saw him. He may come back at any moment. He's still the same asshole. I hope he doesn't annoy you like he has Kyle and me."

"I didn't see him. I'm sure I'll be fine, Lauren. Can I have a glass of water or something?" Owen asked.

Lauren stood up and filled a glass with tap water, not using the Brita filter. After giving it to Owen, Kyle noticed that Owen winked at her.

"You look amazing, Lauren. Are you dating anyone? I didn't see any relationship status on your Facebook profile."

Lauren sat down. "I'm seeing someone. We're getting to know each other. I want to see where it'll go."

Kyle hoped to catch her eye. Instead, she put her hand under the table and held his. "Well, whoever he is, he's a lucky guy. I'm not seeing anyone. Maybe when I get back, I'll start. I may be able to retire within a few years at one of my properties."

"Do you have more than one home?" Kyle asked.

Owen didn't stop staring at Lauren. "I own three: Tennessee, Florida, and Colorado. I hope to sell the Florida and Colorado ones and build a new one in Idaho. I used to have one in Minnesota a few years back, but I sold that before 2008. When I retire, I'll split my time between the two."

"Sounds good. Will you invite us over sometime?" Lauren asked.

Owen finished his water. "I think we can arrange that." He gave her a coy smile.

Lauren grabbed the empty glass and put it in the sink. Owen didn't take his eyes off her. She smiled at Owen and went to her bedroom. To Kyle, her smile seemed fake; it didn't quite meet her eyes.

Owen looked down the hall as she walked away. "She's looking better than ever. If she ever breaks up with that guy she's seeing, I'm jumping in."

"I don't think that's a good idea." Kyle fiddled with his shirt hem.

Owen stood up and grabbed the champagne. "She'll want to be with me if she's single. I've got enough money to make her happy."

Kyle felt his face reddening, so he went to the freezer to cool off, pretending to look for something. He took out two ice cubes, put them in a glass, and filled it with tap water.

"I expect Erica will be here any minute now," Kyle said.

"I'll be interested to see her. I saw her once in our twenties, and she was gorgeous. She was kind of standoffish that day, though. I also thought she was kind of cute in our teens. I knew that behind the zits, there was a nice face."

"I think she liked you back then," Kyle said.

"Now that I think of it, I think you're right. When we went for that walk to Dade Woods years ago, I kept catching her staring at me. Maybe I can get with her if Lauren doesn't give in."

Kyle sipped his water then said, "Just be subtle about it. You weren't so much with Lauren. I think that is why she walked away without saying anything."

Owen raised his eyebrows. "I don't need to be subtle. If she likes guys with money, she'll like me."

The doorbell rang. Kyle walked over to the door with Owen right behind him. Looking through the peephole, he saw Erica. She wore a white blouse, black skirt, and her skin was flawless, like she'd used one of those phone filters to beautify herself. Her black hair looked immaculate with a slight tint of red. Kyle opened the door.

"Kyle!"

"Erica! You look great!"

The two of them embraced. Kyle could feel Owen waiting behind him.

"You do look great, Erica," Owen said. "I'm glad you're here."

"Thank you, Owen. Your face has barely changed."

"Please come in," Kyle said. "Everyone else is here, so that's good."

She quickly hugged Owen and walked inside with her black rolling duffle bag.

"This place brings back memories," she said, her eyes glassy.

Owen picked up her luggage and brought it into the kitchen.

"There are a few free rooms here," said Kyle. "I'm down the hall here, and Lauren is in the room across from me. Alex picked a room upstairs, and there are at least two rooms upstairs."

"I may stay here too if there's enough room," Owen said.

"That'd mean someone will have to sleep in Dave's old room," Kyle said. "I'm not sure if anyone wants to do that."

It then occurred to Kyle that Lauren's room had bunk beds.

"I just remembered, there's a bunk bed in Lauren's room. Erica, do you want to share with her?"

"Sounds great! That'll work if she doesn't mind."

Owen's smile faded. "I'll have to go and see what the other room is like. The one that isn't Dave's. I'll go and check now."

Owen picked up her luggage again and went upstairs. His footsteps were loud as he scaled the stairs.

"Why did he take my luggage upstairs, Kyle?"

Kyle shrugged his shoulders. He had an idea but didn't want to say that Owen was pining to get her to stay upstairs with him. Kyle felt that Owen had a lot of nerve to even think of that. Even if Owen meant for Erica to sleep in the room next to him, that meant that Alex would be without a room.

"Let's go and see the others," Kyle proposed.

The two of them went over to the kitchen, and Lauren suddenly appeared from the hallway.

"It's great to see you, Erica!" Lauren said, hugging her.

"Ditto, Lauren."

A few seconds later, Alex came back into the house via the side door.

"Erica, is that you?" Alex said.

Despite some hesitancy, Erica went over to Alex and hugged him.

"It's good to see you again, Erica,"

"Likewise, Alex."

The four of them all went to the kitchen table and sat down.

"It's great to see all of you," Owen said when he returned.

Owen joined them at the table. This was the first time they had all been together since that rainy November day.

Reunion

"It looks like the Fremont Treehouse Club is back to together," Kyle said with a smile.

"I never really liked the name," Alex said. "It sounds so childish, even back when we made it up."

Erica shook her head. "It does sound sort of lame now, but it didn't back then. It had a special meaning."

"Are we all going to go to the treehouse now?" Lauren asked.

Everyone looked at Kyle. "I think we should do it tonight. Right now, we should all get settled in this house. I'm not even sure who's staying here and who's spending the night somewhere else."

Owen was the first to answer. "I think that I'll stay at one of the motels in Woodbrook. Maybe the Midwesterner Inn. I've always wanted to stay there."

"If you want to stay here, I can stay in the bunk bedroom with Lauren," Erica said to Owen. "That way, you can use the other room that's not Dave's."

Owen twiddled his thumbs. "I think I'll pass. Like I said, I'll try for a hotel or maybe the Midwesterner Inn."

"Suit yourself," Erica said. Kyle wanted to say the exact same thing but was glad she beat him to it.

"I'm fine to share with Erica," Lauren said.

Owen scrunched his nose.

Kyle felt like laughing. The man was a petulant child.

"What about dinner later on?" Erica asked.

"Sounds good," Alex responded, raising his eyebrows.

"Ditto," Lauren added.

"I think it's a good idea," Kyle said. "Where can we go?"

Erica took out her cellphone, her thumbs flicking as she browsed. After a few seconds she said, "There's a fondue place at the edge of town. It replaced Donovan's Steakhouse a few years ago."

She showed everyone the website on her phone. Kyle had never been to a fondue place before and wanted to try it. He loved trying new restaurants.

"Hot Stuff is the name of the place?" Lauren asked.

Erica put her phone on the table. "Yes, I guess that's it. I was in Dallas a few years ago and there was a similar place. I really enjoyed it."

"I'm in," Lauren said.

Kyle and Alex both nodded, but Owen simply crossed his arms, his eyes fixed on the ceiling.

"Shall I make a reservation for 5 pm?" Erica asked.

Everyone but Owen nodded.

"I'll call in a few minutes," Erica said. "I want to take a shower first. Is there one upstairs?"

Kyle pointed towards the stairs, and Erica nodded. Kyle noticed that Alex kept staring at Owen, and that Erica's eyes watered after she looked at the living room. She wiped them with her arm, then went to take a shower. He figured that she saw the urn.

'Are you pouting?" Alex asked Owen.

Owen looked at Alex. "I'm not pouting, dickhead. I just feel awkward with all of us being here."

"Awkward how?" Alex asked.

Owen stood up, went to the front door, and went outside. Alex laughed to himself.

"Try not to agitate him, Alex," Kyle said.

Alex shrugged and raised his eyebrows. "I don't know what his problem is. I'm willing to be civil, but he's pouting. What's he pouting about?"

"Fucked if I know," Kyle replied.

Lauren shrugged her shoulders. "I don't know, either."

The front door was still open. Kyle looked out and saw Owen sitting on the Adirondack chair. A cigarette burned in his hand. Kyle returned to the kitchen.

"Let's just get through tonight," Kyle said to Alex. "After today, we can all go our separate ways."

Alex looked down at the table. Kyle realized he may have sounded harsh.

"I think all of us should get cleaned up and rest a bit," Lauren said.

"Good idea," Kyle said.

Lauren took some keys out of her purse and went to the side door. "I'm going to the store."

"Do you want me to go with you?" Kyle asked.

"I need to go by myself," Lauren said, winking at Kyle. "You stay here and hold down the fort."

Kyle nodded.

"See you later," Alex said.

Kyle sent her a text.

KYLE: I'll miss you while you're gone
LAUREN: Ditto
KYLE: I assume you didn't want to tell Owen about us because he'd get into our business, right?
LAUREN: Exactly. Owen is obviously into me
KYLE: Yes, he is. Now he's pouting about it. He's so transparent
LAUREN: He is
KYLE: I can't wait to be alone with you again

LAUREN: Ditto. I'm going to Walgreens. TTYL

When he put his phone away, Kyle saw Alex staring at him. "What's up, Alex?"

"I'm going to take a nap. Wake me up around four."

"Will do."

After Alex left, Kyle felt his phone buzz with a new text.

ALEX: Can you spot me for dinner tonight?
KYLE: Sure
ALEX: Thanks

Kyle was going to offer to pay for Lauren's dinner, and now he had to pay for Alex. Normally, he wouldn't mind paying, but he gathered Alex expected other people to pay for him most of the time. He really didn't want to exclude him, though. Despite all the tension, Kyle was still glad the five of them were together again. Dave would've been happy about it.

The Restaurant

By the time 5 p.m. came, all of them except Lauren were at the Hot Stuff restaurant. Kyle had texted Lauren to see if she wanted a ride. By about 430, she hadn't responded, so he decided to go ahead without her. Owen and Alex went in Owen's BMW, and Erica went in her car.

Kyle made sure there was an empty seat next to him in the restaurant for when Lauren arrived. More than once, Owen looked over at the empty seat. Kyle was surprised by how much Owen had changed. People do change, but it was as if Owen was not the same person. Back when they were teens, he was confident and, in the present, he seemed to be trying too hard.

"Has anyone talked to Lauren recently?" Owen asked.

Erica shrugged. "She texted me that she was at the store about two hours ago. I haven't heard anything else since."

"Yeah," Kyle said. "I haven't heard anything from her since she left. I think that was over four hours ago."

Owen stood up and pointed at the empty seat. "Do you mind if I sit in that seat? I want to sit next to her when she arrives."

Of course, Kyle didn't want to switch seats. On the other hand, he didn't want to make it look like he and Lauren had something going on between them. "Well, Kyle, what's your answer?" Owen grilled.

"Let's just see where she wants to sit. If you want her to sit next to you, pull up another chair."

"That sounds fair to me," Alex said.

Owen wrinkled his nose and let out a deep breath. "Okay, let's see what happens." He pulled an empty chair from another table and put it beside his.

Kyle could tell that Owen wanted to burst out and say something to him and Alex.

The young waitress came over to take their orders. Kyle noticed Owen was staring at her. The guy clearly didn't have an off switch with women.

"I'll have a Vodka gimlet," Owen said.

"Okay, and for you?" the waitress asked Kyle.

"I'll have any beer that's on tap. Surprise me," Kyle replied.

"Just a water for me," Alex said.

"And I'll have a red wine, please," Erica said.

The waitress looked back at Kyle and gave a flirty smile. "Be right back for the main orders."

"Ahh, I think that she might like you, Kyle," Alex said.

Kyle felt his face going red. "It doesn't matter. I'm seeing someone anyways."

"Can you tell us about her?" Erica said.

"Yeah, tell us!" Alex shouted. A few other patrons looked their way.

Before Kyle could say anything, he saw Lauren enter the restaurant. He waved her over.

As she approached the table, Kyle noticed that she was now wearing a white blouse and black skirt. She reminded him of one of the secretaries at work. It was a new side of her that he enjoyed.

"Sorry I'm a bit late. I explored Woodbrook and did some shopping. I bought some new clothes."

Kyle waited to see if she'd sit next to Owen or him. He was delighted when she chose a chair next to him. Owen rolled his eyes.

"The waitress came by and asked us what we wanted for drinks. We weren't sure what you wanted," Erica said.

"I think I'll just have some water. I stay away from sugary drinks, and I've never been a fan of alcohol, at least not for the last ten years or so."

The waitress came back with their drinks, and all of them ordered. They each got one of the platters. Kyle got the seafood with a salad, Lauren got the vegetarian platter, Alex and Owen both ordered the steak and chicken, and Erica ordered the surf and turf.

As they ate, Kyle learned That Owen would probably be able to retire by the age of forty, and that he had a vast stock portfolio. There was no subtlety in the way that he made himself look well off. Erica said that she was a part-time model, and that she also worked as a vet tech. The veterinarian that she worked for was one of the best in Florida.

Lauren said that she'd once worked at a bar in St. Louis that the professional football team used to frequent. It was news to him that she'd ever lived in St. Louis.

Alex mentioned his time as a carpenter and then, out of nowhere, blurted out that he had been arrested a few times. He said that he'd had a few DUIs and that one time, he'd got into a fight at a bowling alley and had been in jail for two nights until his dad bailed him out. This was all in his early twenties. Not long after he'd been bailed out, Alex moved away from home and didn't speak to his father for three years.

The dinner conversation went smoothly, and Kyle spotted Owen leering at Lauren several times. Thankfully, Lauren didn't notice. Despite the meal being over two hours long, Kyle felt it went by in half the time.

Just before the waitress brought the checks, Owen said to her, "I'll take the bill on this one."

"You don't need to," Erica said.

"I insist," Owen said. "I've been doing well lately."

"I've no problem with it," Alex said.

Kyle didn't want Owen to pay his bill. It was obvious that Owen was just trying to show off his wealth. While Owen took his credit card from his wallet, he looked right at Lauren. She looked down at the table.

"I really don't mind. I think that I can splurge a little."

Less than a minute later, the waitress came back with the credit card in her hand. "This credit card was rejected. It's probably some mistake by your bank. Do you have any other cards on you?"

Owen's face turned red as he pulled another card from his wallet. He handed it to the waitress, but she soon returned. "I'm sorry to tell you that this one was rejected, too."

"I'll cover it," Kyle said as he handed his credit card to the waitress.

"I don't know what to say," said Owen, hanging his head. "This has never happened to me before. I feel so embarrassed. I have the funds."

Kyle was glad to see Owen cut down to size. Normally, he was not one to see someone embarrassed, but Owen had been rubbing him the wrong way. He wondered if the others at the table felt the same way.

"It's no problem. I had a big lawsuit a few months ago that paid pretty decently," Kyle said.

Owen let out a sigh. "I'll get it next time. I think that all of us should get together like this again."

The total bill was over four hundred dollars, so Kyle gave the waitress a hundred-dollar tip. She noticed the tip right away and thanked Kyle. Right after she left, Kyle saw Owen staring at him, fidgeting in his chair.

"Shall we go back to the treehouse now?" Erica asked.

Without a word, Owen stood up and went to the waitress at the front of the restaurant, the four of them watching him.

"What's up with him?" Alex asked.

"Something isn't right with his cards," Erica said.

Alex laughed. "I have an idea what's going on with them. He's broke! I noticed he hasn't got any cash in his wallet. You would think that someone in his position would carry cash."

"What do you mean?" Lauren asked.

Before Alex could respond, shouting came from the front of the restaurant. "What do you mean this one is rejected too? That's impossible! Your credit card machine sucks!"

The front door slammed. Kyle quickly stood and saw the waitress looked glassy-eyed, her hands shaking.

Kyle went over to her. "What happened with him?" he asked.

She wiped her eyes. "He had me try two more of his cards on your bill, and they also got rejected. He told me to not use your cash. When his card didn't work, he stormed off. I was afraid he was going to crack the glass on the door; he slammed it so hard."

Kyle looked out the front door and saw Owen speeding out of the parking lot in his BMW, wheels screeching.

"I guess we won't see him for at least a few hours," Lauren said from behind Kyle.

Kyle turned around. Alex and Erica were there, too. "He's acting like a hothead. It's best to just let him cool off."

"I agree," Erica said. "He needs to calm down. If that means we have to wait until tomorrow to all meet in the treehouse, so be it."

In the Meantime

Kyle left the restaurant first. He made sure that Alex was distracted by asking him to go with Erica to see if there were any decent movies on at the Redbox across the street by the Walgreens. If Owen had gone back to Dave's house, Kyle would have the best chance of settling him down, and Alex would only make things worse. Kyle felt confident he could beat Lauren home.

A few minutes later, he parked in front of Dave's house. Owen's BWM was nowhere to be seen. Kyle didn't know if he should go around Woodbrook to look for him or stay put. After thinking about it, he decided to stay at the house.

He got out of his car, looked across the street, and saw Mr. Walsh walking his dachshund. Mr. Walsh had a cane, and his back was arched. His gray hair overlapped his ears; he clearly hadn't had a haircut in months.

"Is that you, Mr. Brighton?"

Kyle was pleased that Mr. Walsh remembered him. "Yes, it is, Mr. Walsh. How are you doing?"

"Please come here to me," Mr. Walsh said, gesturing.

Lauren hadn't got back yet, so Kyle rushed across the street to Mr. Walsh.

"I recognized you; you look so much like your father," Mr. Walsh said. "How are your parents doing nowadays?"

"They're in Madison. I'm living in Cincinnati right now. I work as an attorney."

Mr. Walsh smiled with nostalgia. "Well, that's good to hear. My wife passed away two years ago. It's just me and my dog Rascal here. He keeps me company."

"I'm sorry to hear that, Mr. Walsh."

"Thank you for your condolences, Kyle. Would you like to join me for a beer inside? I've some new ones that I picked up yesterday."

Kyle looked down the street and saw Lauren's car heading their way. "I'm not free tonight, but I can stop by tomorrow. I'll be staying at Dave's for at least a few days."

"I heard about his passing. Simply awful news. He was a good guy. He offered to mow my lawn and assist me with other chores. I never got around to asking him for help, though. Are you housesitting David's place?"

"Yes, my friends are here too. They'll be here for at least one more day."

Mr. Walsh started to walk back to his house. Once he arrived at his front door, he turned around. "Please stop by tomorrow if you can. A lot has changed around here in the last eight to ten years. I'll tell you all about it. Have a good night."

Kyle waved to Mr. Walsh and waited for Lauren to park her car. At the far end of the street, he saw a car stop at the sign for a few seconds before continuing. It looked like the same BMW Owen had rented.

"Was that Owen that was down the street?" Kyle asked Lauren, pointing.

"If it was, I didn't see him following me. It would be creepy if he did."

Kyle put out his hand, and she took it as she exited her car. "I guess we need to keep our new relationship secret from the others now. That's what you want, right?"

Lauren pursed her lips. "Yes, I don't want Owen or anyone else trying to mess it up. Alex has a big mouth. I wouldn't want him to say anything to Owen or to piss you off."

"I understand. Owen has been trying to get with you. I think he was trying to impress you back at the restaurant, but it backfired. I guess all his credit cards failed. That's very odd. I don't know what to make of that."

"Do you think he uses fake or stolen credit cards, Kyle?"

That was something that Kyle hadn't thought of. Either way, something was certainly amiss.

"Not sure, and I'm not sure I want to know right now. I won't bring it up when I see him."

"I don't really want to be alone with him. I'm afraid he might try to put a move on me. I was thinking about it on the drive back here."

Kyle gently led her towards the porch. "If we all get together in the treehouse tomorrow, I've got a feeling he'll leave after that. His ego seems bruised. Until then, stay around either me, Erica, or Alex at any time. Don't be alone with him."

As the two of them walked up to the porch, Erica arrived and parked next to Lauren. The second she turned off the car, she opened her door and ran to the porch.

"Is everything okay?" Kyle asked.

"I texted Owen before I left the restaurant. Here are the texts he sent me." Erica showed her phone to Kyle.

ERICA: Are you going back to the house?

OWEN: Not right now. The four of you can enjoy being together

ERICA: Will you come back?

OWEN: Don't know. I'll decide later

ERICA: Stay safe

OWEN: Like you care

After Kyle read the texts, he handed the phone over to Lauren so she could read them.

"I hope he just needs some time to blow off steam," Kyle said.

"Yeah, he may just need that," Lauren said, handing the phone back to Erica.

Kyle looked at his phone and saw that Erica had called him a few minutes earlier. "Sorry I missed your call. Was it about Owen?"

Erica nodded.

Alex was still sitting in Erica's car, so Kyle waved him over. He got out of the car and walked towards them, but he clearly wasn't in a hurry.

"What if he doesn't come back to join us?" Lauren asked. "Will we still get together in the treehouse?"

Kyle sighed. "We promised to all get together if the circle was broken. I hope that Owen will keep that promise. After all, he did show up here on short notice."

"I hope you're right," Erica said, putting her phone in her purse.

Lauren sat down on one of the porch steps. "I need to tell all of you something that happened before between Owen and me."

Kyle's heart dropped. Her tone wasn't reassuring. Kyle sat beside her, and Erica and Alex stood in front of them.

"We're listening," Erica said.

"About a year ago, Owen started to contact me after he found me on Facebook. We started talking on the phone. We even met up as he lives maybe fifteen miles from me."

"Did something happen?" Erica asked, sitting on the other side of Lauren.

Lauren's eyes widened. "He once made a pass at me. It's not a big deal, as I told him I didn't want anything to happen between us. The truth is I've never wanted it. I just wanted to be his friend. His ego couldn't take that."

"Was there more that happened?" Erica asked.

"Yes." Lauren awkwardly scratched the back of her neck. "We didn't meet up again, but he texted me all the time. I was polite, so he kept doing it. It went on for like two months. I would get hundreds of texts a day from him. I'd reply sometimes, but it was too much. I stopped responding one day, and he kept texting me for three days straight. I counted something like two hundred texts without me answering."

"Was that the end of it?" Kyle asked.

Lauren shook her head and put her hands on her face. "No, the texting started up about a week later. I finally texted back to tell him to give me some space."

Kyle put his arm around her shoulder. He wanted to kiss her but knew she didn't want the others knowing about their relationship.

Alex joined them on the steps. "Was that the end of it?"

"Nope," Lauren said, removing her hands from her face, her eyes welling. "I was stupid and texted back every so often. A few weeks later, I told him that I had a boyfriend. The truth was I didn't. I just couldn't have him bothering me anymore.

"That's creepy," Alex quipped.

"I almost blocked Owen on my phone, but I'm glad I didn't. He texted me right before Kyle contacted me to tell me about Dave. I might not have answered the phone if Owen didn't tell me. I sometimes don't answer calls from unknown numbers."

"Yeah, it actually worked out," Kyle remarked.

"Are you seeing anyone now?" Erica asked.

Kyle squeezed her shoulder, nervous about what she would say. He passed her a Kleenex from his pocket. After dabbing her eyes, she gave a forced smile.

"I'm seeing someone. I just met him recently. I've known him for a long time. I'm going to see how it goes. Earlier today, I told Owen I was seeing someone, and he didn't seem to respect that, telling me that I need a real man."

Alex sighed. "He kept staring at you during dinner. I was going to rip on him, but I'm glad I didn't. I think it would have made things worse."

"I wish that I'd known this," Erica said, then looked up, distracted by something down the street.

Kyle stood to see the same BMW from earlier crossing the far end of the street. This time, it stopped in the middle of the road for a few seconds before pulling away in a hurry.

"I believe that's him," Kyle said in a low voice.

"I think so, too," Erica said. "It's freaking me out."

Alex pulled his phone out of his pocket. "Maybe I should text him. Even I'm freaked out about his behavior. He seems unhinged over something so minor."

"Let's wait a few minutes," Kyle said. "We can pretend we didn't see him."

Erica grabbed Lauren's hand and gently pulled her off the porch's steps. "I'll take Lauren inside. Maybe the two of you can stay out here and text Owen."

"Good idea," Kyle said.

The two women went inside the house. Alex stared at them as they walked away. He shook his head and smirked to himself.

"What're you smirking at, Alex?"

"Both of them are so fucking hot! I'd love to get with either of them."

Kyle felt like slapping Alex. "Lauren said that she's with someone. Respect that. Don't start acting like Owen. Also, don't you still have a thing for Erica?"

"I drove home from the restaurant with her, didn't I?"

"That means nothing, Alex."

Alex stuck out his middle finger at Kyle and bit his lower lip for a quick second. "Well, we had a conversation in the car."

"And what was discussed?"

"We admitted that we both had feelings for each other when we were younger. I did talk shit about her years ago, and I said I was sorry. She also admitted talking shit about me, too. We called it even."

"That's all you talked about, Alex?"

Alex looked at the front door to make sure no one was listening to them. "Me and her are probably going to meet up later tonight. When I say that, I mean maybe in one of the bedrooms here."

After looking up at the door again, Alex pulled out a blunt and lit up. Kyle hated the smell of it, so he covered his mouth with his hand. Alex shook his head but didn't say anything.

"If you like Erica, I suggest you stick to her and don't make any comments about Lauren," said Kyle.

Alex threw the blunt on the grass and stepped on it. "I guess you're right. Erica would probably get really jealous."

"Since you've talked, do you think Erica wants anything serious? If she doesn't, do you?" Kyle asked.

Alex shrugged. "Right now, I don't want anything more than a hook up. I think she wants the same thing. If not, then that's not my problem."

Kyle wanted to tell Alex that his attitude towards Erica's feelings was unkind. On the other hand, she was a grown woman who could weigh the options herself. Kyle figured keeping silent about the situation was best.

Just as Kyle was about to go back inside, he noticed the same BMW coming down the road with its headlights on. As it got closer, it didn't seem to slow down. Alex noticed the car, too. The car braked and looked like it was going to mount the sidewalk and hit the fire hydrant. Luckily, it screeched to a halt unscathed.

"It's Owen in that car!" Alex yelled to Kyle.

Owen got out of the car, a scowl on his face. They went over to him.

"How's it going, buddy?" Alex asked.

Owen pursed his lips. "I needed to do some thinking. I got a room at the Midwesterner Inn. I'll be there for one or two nights. After that, I'm probably going home."

"Will you be here tomorrow for the treehouse?" Kyle asked.

"Yes, I'll be here for that. How about around seven tomorrow night?"

Kyle looked at Alex, and they both nodded.

"Great, I'll be back here around six thirty tomorrow. I've got a few errands to do around town," Owen said.

Without saying goodbye, Owen got back into the car and drove off in a hurry. In a way, Kyle was glad that Owen would be gone most of the day tomorrow. That way, he wouldn't have to deal with Owen and could visit Mr. Walsh. There was also the option of driving around Woodbrook to see what had changed.

"I'm going in, Alex. Are you staying out here for a bit?"

Alex nodded. "I'll probably take a walk around the block or something. I need some fresh air."

Kyle waved at Alex, who simply turned and walked away up the street.

"Time has changed so much," Kyle said to himself before going into the house.

The Kitchen

Once Kyle entered the house, he saw Erica sitting at the kitchen table, staring into space, a blue ceramic cup in her hand. Kyle looked in the TV room and the living room for Lauren, but she wasn't there.

"Where's Lauren?" Kyle asked Erica.

She looked up. "She's in her room. She got a call a few minutes ago and went there. I don't know who she's talking to."

More mystery. Hopefully, it wasn't some ex-boyfriend or someone who'd wreck her emotional state.

"Do the two of you have plans tonight?" Kyle asked.

Erica shook her head. "I think I'll just go to bed early. I want to see if Owen comes back, though. After that, I'm not sure."

Kyle sat down at the table across from Erica. "I saw him a few minutes ago. He's going to stay at the Midwesterner Inn."

"Maybe that's a good thing, Kyle. I used to have him on Facebook a while back. I unfriended him as he would send me messages on there almost every day. A few times, he hinted at a date. I never took the bait."

Kyle remembered that Owen mentioned to him that she'd unfriended him. Now he knew why.

"He'll be back tomorrow night so we can all gather at the treehouse."

"Sounds good. Where's Alex?"

"He decided to take a walk around the block. Are you doing anything with him tonight?"

She looked down at the cup. Her mouth opened, but nothing came out.

"Did you want to say something, Erica?"

"Yes, Kyle. I wanted to mention that I'm sorry that I lost touch with you within the last few years. I seemed to lose touch with a few people then. I shut myself off with some people for a few months and then couldn't get the nerve to contact them back after that. Work was bad and I had a breakup with a boyfriend at the time. I know if was stupid, but it really shut me down. I still haven't spoken with a few people since then. I should start again once I get back home. I know that I have the strength to do that.

"Agreed. It's not too late."

Kyle went to the fridge to see if there was anything new in it. To his surprise, there was now a six-pack of Coors beer, a gallon of cranberry juice, and a two-liter of Coke. All of them looked good, but in the end, he took one of the beer cans.

"Did you get these drinks?" Chris asked Erica while pointing at the fridge.

"Yes, I got on the way here form the airport."

"Any plans?" he asked Erica again.

"I'm not sure," she responded. "Me and Alex talked about doing something tonight. Not sure if I really want to, though."

'Why not?" Kyle asked, joining her at the table.

"I've mixed feelings, Kyle. I used to have a crush on him years ago. This was before I'd heard he'd talked shit about me. Those feelings do die hard, though. I wanted to give him another try. Thinking about it, I'm starting to wonder if I should just keep him at a distance. I've heard bad things about him, such as DUIs but I'm trying to forget that. I don't really want to explain the other bad things I've heard. They may not be true."

"I need to ask; what exactly did you want to do with him tonight?" Kyle wanted to see if what Alex had told him was accurate.

"Well, I figured that he wants to get with me. It sounds fun, but I may regret it, Kyle. I was with him for a short bit in high school, but that was back then. I'm looking for some sort of commitment right now, not a one-night stand."

"I see," Kyle responded.

"What do you think, Kyle?"

Kyle wanted to tell the truth and that he thought Erica hooking up with Alex wasn't a good idea. Alex didn't want any commitment. Also, the DUIs were definitely true, and she shouldn't ignore that. On the other hand, Kyle didn't want to ruin

Alex's chances or get involved. Pissing Alex off would be a bad move.

"It's up to you. It's your life, Erica. It didn't work in high school. Maybe it will be the same now. Maybe it won't. We're adults now so thing could be different. You decide. If you feel it isn't right, maybe you shouldn't get involved with Alex."

Erica smiled. "Why does Lauren get to have the good one?"

Kyle now figured that Lauren had told Erica about them. He decided to play dumb. "What do you mean?"

"She told me, Kyle. I know that she doesn't want Alex or Owen to know. I won't tell them. Owen is after her, and Alex can't keep a secret. I think it's great you two are together. She needs a change in her life."

"Why do you think she needs a change?" Kyle asked, hoping Erica might reveal something about Lauren he didn't know yet.

Erica tapped the cup with her finger. "She hasn't had that much luck over the past few years. Her son's father is a deadbeat. She had a good relationship a short while back, but it turned sour. There's also the unfortunate event with her ovaries. You know about that last part, right?"

Kyle shook his head.

"Oh shit!" Erica said, covering her mouth.

The issue with her ovaries must've been the secret that Lauren didn't want to tell him about. Kyle had mentioned to her that he wanted kids, and that must've made her feel awful. If he had known her issue, he never would've said anything like that to her. He had to know if that was her secret.

"Can she not have any more kids?"

Erica looked around to make sure Lauren wasn't nearby. "Yes, that's an issue. She had to have them removed due to medical complications. I guess it was about a year or so ago. I only found out about it this morning. She called me when I was at the airport. She also told me that you met up at the park and kissed. I figured she might've told you about her health stuff then."

Kyle nodded. "I'm glad you told me. It takes a big weight off my mind. I thought the secret was something else, not sure what, though. Still, what happened to her was terrible. It has no bearing on how I feel about her, though."

"Will you tell her that I told you?" Erica asked.

Kyle cracked open the beer but suddenly realized he didn't want it. "I'll see if she can tell me. If I think it becomes too difficult, I might tell her."

Erica reached across the table and touched his hand. "I feel that you'll do what's right. You seem like the only sane guy here. She's very lucky." Erica pulled her hand anyway.

"I feel bad for her," Kyle said. "This has probably been burning inside her since we kissed. I wanted to know what was bothering her, but she told me to not ask. I stepped back after that. I feel bad for asking and wanting to know."

"Any person would want to know. That's normal. I think that you handled it the right way. She told me something about you."

"What did she say?" Kyle asked.

Erica finished drinking what was in her cup and put it back on the table. "She said it was a miracle that she met up with you when she did. If she'd come here later, she wouldn't have had that precious time in the park with you. She said it was almost as if it was meant to be."

"I guess it was good timing," Kyle said. "I just wish the circumstances with Dave's death had been different."

"I wish that too, Kyle."

Kyle remembered Dave's ashes. "I was told that Dave wanted me to do something with his ashes. I'm not sure what, though. Do you know?"

Erica nodded her head.

Lauren entered the kitchen. "Sorry I was gone for a bit. I needed to talk to my ex-husband."

"Is everything alright, Lauren?" Kyle asked.

"It is now. My ex was complaining that I was here. Taylor keeps asking for me, so I'll be going home the day after next."

Kyle wished that she was staying longer, but he understood the situation. Her having a child wasn't an issue for him, but it was something that he'd need to get used to.

"I'm glad you were able to come. We'll be able to fulfill Dave's wish," Kyle said.

Lauren walked over to Kyle and kissed him on the cheek. "I'm also glad that I was reunited with you."

After smiling at Erica, Lauren walked out of the kitchen towards her bedroom. After she disappeared from sight, he stared down the hall and realized how lucky he was to meet up with her again. He didn't really believe in fate, but the idea was starting to look more realistic.

"I've something else to tell you," Erica said.

"Go ahead."

"Because of you, she now has a new outlook on life. She told me that."

"A better one?"

"Of course. Your time together in the park made her feel young and carefree again. No one in her life has ever had that effect on her. She wants to tell you this but isn't sure how. You really hit the mark with her."

"That's nice to hear, Erica. I've never felt like I've made an impact on anyone before." He couldn't help smiling.

Erica stood and put her cup in the sink. "I'm kind of jealous. I've never had that kind of experience before. I've tried to find it, but no luck."

Kyle wanted to tell Erica that Alex wasn't right for what she wanted. He tried to think of a subtle way to tell her, but nothing came to mind. Instead, he just nodded.

"Is she going to sleep in your room tonight?" Erica asked.

Kyle's face turned red. "I don't think so, not with all you guys around. I want that time to be special."

"Jealous again, Kyle. Why can't a guy like me for more than my looks?"

"You just need to find the right guy who likes you for the right reason."

"And it isn't Alex, right?"

Kyle paused, staring at his beer, afraid of making eye contact and revealing his true feelings on the subject. Eventually, he looked at Erica, hoping she could read what was on his mind.

"That's up to you, Erica. Go with your heart."

Erica's eyes watered. "It's not that easy. Maybe it is for you, but not for me. You have a good start with Lauren. I've nothing right now."

Judging by Erica's reaction, Kyle wondered if there was a deeper issue with her. She was attractive, so she wouldn't struggle for attention. Her personality wasn't too boisterous, and she wasn't shy. There had to be some other reason why she wasn't meeting the type of men she wanted to.

"I didn't mean to make you upset," Kyle said. "Maybe you should think about what or who can fulfill your needs. After you figure that out, see if you can fulfill the needs of the men you're interested in. Only you can figure that out."
She wiped away her tears with the back of her hand. "I guess I'll need to think about that."

Kyle wondered if she had just been thinking of her own needs. If that's what she'd been doing, then it made a lot of sense. It seemed like common sense to him, but he also knew that not everyone thought like he did.

"I'll consider what you said. I'm going to my room for a while, Kyle. I'll be in one of the empty rooms upstairs. If you see Alex, please tell him I need to be alone tonight. Hopefully he understands.

"Will do."

She walked away, and Kyle hoped he hadn't made her feel worse. Deep inside, he regretted saying anything. Hopefully, all would be better once morning came.

The Porch

Just as Kyle was about to go to his bedroom, he heard a noise on the front porch. He hurried outside and saw Alex sitting on the Adirondack chair with his eyes were closed, Kyle decided to not say anything. The sun was almost down, but the porch light wasn't on. The sound of the chirruping crickets seemed like the perfect white noise to doze off with. He looked at his watch and saw it was now after nine.

"Have a good rest," Kyle said softly.

"I'm not asleep," Alex groaned as Kyle was about to go back inside.

Kyle stepped closer to Alex, and that's when he saw it. Alex had an inch-long scratch on his face with a small trickle of blood running down his cheek.

"Alex, are you okay?" Alex groaned again. "Are you drunk?" Kyle asked.

Alex opened his eyes. "I'm not. I just tripped over the chair. I'm really tired. I thought I might just sleep out here for a bit."

"You might catch a cold out here. I think it's supposed to get down to the low sixties tonight."

"Don't worry about me," Alex said, waving his hand tas if swatting away Kyle's words. "You can just go inside and be with yourself. I'll be fine here."

Kyle sat down on the other Adirondack chair. "Did you see anything interesting on your walk?"

Alex closed his eyes again. After a minute, Kyle figured Alex was asleep, so he stood up.

"Sit back down, Kyle. I'm not asleep, just drowsy."

"I think there's something wrong with you," Kyle said, sitting back down. "You don't seem yourself."

Alex put his hand over his face. "You know that I've been a fuckup almost all my life. Well...that's still me. I'm a fuckup. I'm going nowhere...and I wish I could change that. I see someone like you and wish I could be like that. I wish that I could even be like Owen. That is, Owen without the gut."

Kyle tried not to laugh, but he couldn't keep it in.

"I lied to you. I told you on the phone the other day that I was waiting for the right price for my carpentry work. That was...not the truth, Kyle."

"What's the truth, Alex?"

Alex took his hand off his face. "The truth is that I once did a job for a guy who lived near me, and he tried to screw me over with my pay. His mistake was telling me he would pay me a certain amount before I finished, and then he told me a different amount, so I left a few things unfinished. One of them was wiring a ceiling light. He only found out about it the next day. I was already paid, so it didn't matter to me."

"What happened next?"

"I was set up to do a lot of work for people around my neighborhood. Word got around that I'd screwed him over, so no one wanted to hire me anymore. I tried to go to my dad for money, but he wouldn't give me any. I really screwed myself. I should've just done a good job for that guy, then never worked for him again."

Kyle did feel sorry for Alex in a way, but on the other hand, he didn't. Alex had always had a temper that got the best of him. Sure, the guy who screwed him with the money was wrong, but it could've been handled differently.

"How long ago was that?" Kyle asked.

"It was about three months ago. I started making tables and chairs for people and selling them on Facebook. I made a bit of money at first, but someone must've said something bad about me; I don't know who. Almost overnight, I didn't get any inquiries about my furniture. I made good stuff, too."

Kyle thought that Alex might ask him for more money.

"I'm sorry to hear that, Alex. Maybe you should move to another area and start over. Go to a place where no one knows you."

Alex sat up and brought his knees to his chest. "I've thought of that. I don't have the money to move right now, though. I wouldn't have been able to get here without your help. I had maybe twenty bucks on me when I got to Woodbrook. I wasted all of that at Rafferty's bar the other night."

Kyle had forgotten that Alex had gone right to the bar after the train.

"Were you drunk when you were there? I texted you, and it took you a long time to respond. And you slept outside."

"Oh yeah, I was drunk. I told you I passed out, but I never said why. Too many shots and double bourbons."

Kyle knew so many drinks would add up to much more than twenty dollars.

"Did someone buy you some drinks, Alex?"

Kyle noticed Alex's right hand was shaking. "Leave me alone. I don't need any lectures. My dad still gives them to me, and I don't want to hear any from you guys while I'm here."

Kyle wanted answers but decided to leave Alex alone. After a few minutes of silence, Alex started to snore. Leaving Alex outside was probably the best thing to do if he was in a bad mood, so Kyle went in and took a blanket from the couch in the TV room. Without waking him, Kyle put it over Alex. Kyle wasn't ready to go to sleep yet. He would check on Alex in an hour or so. To pass the time, he watched TV. The Cincinnati Reds were playing the San Diego Padres. Watching that game would be a good distraction for the next hour or so.

The Basement Discovery

The game was so boring that Kyle fell asleep. When he woke, it was dark outside. He looked at his watch; it was a little after midnight. Rubbing his eyes, he turned off the TV and looked outside. Alex was no longer there, and neither was the blanket.

Kyle didn't feel like going back to sleep, so he went to the fridge and took out a Coke. After chugging down the whole can, he crushed it with his hand and threw it into the trash. Since everyone appeared to be asleep, Kyle didn't know what to do. After looking into Lauren's bedroom and seeing her asleep, he decided that maybe the basement was a good place to go, as he wouldn't have to be so quiet down there.

Once he'd climbed down the basement steps, he looked around for something to keep him busy. He couldn't play music on the CD player again without waking everyone. Watching the old eighties-style TV would probably put him back to sleep, and playing darts wasn't any fun alone. Then he remembered there was a small room that he didn't go into earlier. Back when they were kids, it was where Dave used to keep all his board games and toys.

Kyle opened the door to the room and couldn't find a light fixture on the wall. He used the flashlight on his cellphone and saw a chain switch hanging from a lightbulb. After pulling the chain, the light was so bright that Kyle dropped his cellphone.

The room was full of boxes and books on shelves. Cobwebs hung on the walls and shelves. One of the boxes had Dave's name on it. Kyle didn't want to pry but was curious to see if something in it might bring back memories.

Inside the box were a few yearbooks from his time in junior high and high school. Kyle remembered signing Dave's senior yearbook, so he picked it up and sat on the floor. A layer of dust caked the yearbook, so Kyle blew on it. The dust got into his eyes and mouth. He used his shirt to wipe the rest of it off.

He couldn't remember where he'd signed, and after a few minutes of turning pages, he started to lose interest. After closing the book and standing up, a piece of paper fell out of the book and onto the floor. Without any hesitation, Kyle picked it up and put the yearbook back in the box.

Normally, Kyle wouldn't normally snoop at what the paper said, but he felt it was fair game since it had fallen out of the book.

Dave,

I'm so sad that high school will be ending soon. I'll miss math class with you and Steve. Only two weeks left! I really enjoyed our time as friends. I'm sorry I wasn't able to spend as much time with you and the others. My mother got strict after I got a little drunk in my friend's basement. What was I thinking? A year or so before that, I refused to get into a car with Lucy Bachman when she was drunk. I'm not sure if you remember her but she graduated two years ago.

Anyhoo, did you ever talk to Kyle about all of us getting together again? I've had a crush on him ever since we all got together in the treehouse. I think he doesn't seem to realize it, though. I wish that the six of us could get together again there soon. That time was very important to all of us. It made me feel like I was part of something special.

-L

The note felt like a treasure, and Kyle wanted to keep it but knew it wasn't his to keep. He put it back in the middle of the yearbook.

Once he'd put the yearbook back in the box again, he wondered if there were any other notes that Dave and Lauren had exchanged. There were some other pieces of folded paper at the bottom of the box, so he took them out. There were five in total.

Two of them were notes from someone named Kevin, so Kyle put those back. Two others were from a girl named Lucy, so those went back in the box too. The last one was another one from Lauren, so he sat down again to read it.

Dave,

Can't believe that we've only got two days left of school! I'll miss passing notes. It's something that I'll never forget. It's amazing that Mr. Waterman never caught us passing these.

 Did you talk to Kyle about me? If so, what did he say? I'm buggin' to find out. I didn't have a chance to really talk to him this semester. I wish I was in a class with him like we're in this one. I saw him in the hall the other day, and he waved. I wish I could at least talk to him on the phone, but my mom won't let me. That's so stupid, right?

 Do you know anything about this Y2K thing? It scares me. I should be home from college then, so at least I'll be home.

 What are you doing for the Fourth of July? Maybe I can convince my mom to let me go with you and the others in the FTC. Whatcha think? I turn 18 in August, so there's not much my mom can tell me to do after that. Booyah!

               -L

Kyle's hands shook when he finished the letter. He couldn't remember Dave telling him anything about Lauren. When they were teens, Dave had told him everything. It was highly unlikely that he would've forgotten. There had to be more to it, as Kyle had seen Dave several times after graduation. He was even at Dave's graduation party. Did Dave not say anything to him about Lauren liking him on purpose?

Kyle dropped the letter back into the box. He was now curious to see if anything else was connected to him in the other boxes. The first two boxes had old school papers that belonged to Dave. Nothing of interest in there. The next box had some old, wrinkled comics that looked like they'd been wet at some time. The box after that had dozens of photographs. Many of them were damaged as if they'd gotten wet like the comics. One picture was of graduation, and it had Dave, Kyle, and Erica in it by Dave's fireplace. Kyle decided to put that one in his pocket.

The last box was the most interesting. It contained several spiral notebooks, each of them blue with the initials DF scrawled on them in black marker. There were seven in total. Kyle first thought about not looking at them, but there was also the idea that something was written about himself in there. Kyle opened the one on the top and saw handwritten journal entries. The one that he opened started with the date 7-12-1994. By taking a quick glance, he saw that this mentioned Dave's family vacation to Mexico. Such events didn't interest him. Kyle remembered that it was about a year before they all met in the treehouse. He skipped to the final entry, which was dated 3-14-1995.

He searched through the others, looking for one that might include something about their night in the treehouse. Soon, he found one dated 3-22-1995. He skipped to the middle until he found 8-20-1995.

8-22-1995

Dear Diary,

A few days ago, I met up with some of my friends in the treehouse. My parents were having a block party, and a bunch of us got bored, so I wanted to show off the treehouse. There were six of us: Alex, Erica, Lauren, Owen, Kyle, and, of course, myself. We formed a club (FTC) and made a pact. FTC means Fremont Treehouse Club. The name is kind of lame, but its what we agreed on. I can't even write what the pact was about in case others read it here. I'm glad that we formed that club. I hope to meet up with them again soon. We shared some details with each other that made me feel like I'm part of something special. I've never felt that way before. I hope that the others felt that way.

Kyle enjoyed reading that entry, as Dave not only mentioned the FTC, but he didn't reveal details about their pact. Kyle went to the next entry.

9-2-1995

Dear Diary,

School is back. I'm in some classes with my friends, but it hasn't started off all that well. I tried to go on a date with Lauren from the FTC, but her mother wouldn't let her go. I'm afraid to ask again. I think that maybe we should just be friends. There's another cute girl in my Advanced Algebra class. Her name is Teresa. I may just ask her if she wants to go to Homecoming with me. If she says no, I may not go at all. I don't want to be rejected more than once.

I hope my grades don't slip this year. I'm hoping to go to Northwestern. Kyle also wants to go there. My parents would be very disappointed if I didn't get in to somewhere like there.

Kyle wanted to read more. He didn't know that Dave had been interested in Lauren. That was why Dave hadn't told him about how Lauren felt. Even though it was a long time ago, and Dave was gone, it was hard not to be mad with him. Kyle thought about all the years he and Lauren had potentially missed out on as a couple.

10-14-1995

Dear Diary,

I didn't go to Homecoming with Teresa. She went with some guy I'd never heard of. I wound up not going. My grades are staying strong, so that's good. Luckily, Lauren hasn't been acting weird since I asked her on a date. I wonder if I should ask her again.

Kyle had to read the next entry.

10-22-1995

Dear Diary,

I'm a chickenshit. I had the chance to ask Lauren out again, but I didn't. I saw her in the hall at school. She was on the payphone and I was walking towards her. I had a chance and screwed it up. Maybe I'll wait a few weeks. I could use the excuse of getting all the FTC people together in the treehouse, but then I wouldn't be alone with her. I don't know what to do.

Kyle remembered that the walk they all took was the next month, so he wanted to read the next entry.

11-16-1995

Dear Diary,

I've planned an outing with all the members of the FTC. It was one of the only ways I could get Lauren to meet with me. Hopefully, we will have some time to talk. We're going to Dade Woods. It won't be a meeting in the treehouse, but at least we'll all be together. I think that Kyle likes her. I saw him staring at her a bunch in the treehouse a few months back. If he does, maybe there's a chance that she likes him back. If he does like her, I won't try to bother them. Let's see what happens.

Kyle quickly read the next entry.

12-2-1995

Dear Diary,

The trip the FTC had to Dade Woods was good and bad. It was good because I got the chance to spend some quality time with my friends. I'll never forget that. It was bad because Kyle was with Lauren a lot, so I couldn't get her alone. The reason I didn't want to go into the treehouse was that it wouldn't give me a chance to talk to Lauren one-on-one. Kyle monopolized her. I think they both like each other. I don't know what he would do if Lauren's mom prevented her from seeing him. Maybe it was a good thing that I didn't get to know her better. Her mom would have kept preventing us from going on dates. I invited her to a party I'm having in two weeks, but she can't go. What a bummer!

On another note, I recently had a relative die and they wanted to be cremated. To me, that's so odd. I can't fathom what it would be like to not have a body in a grave. This has been a morbid thought that I've had since then. It's bothering me.

The next entry read.

1-9-1996.
Dear Diary,

The party didn't happen on December 16th. My parents were supposed to be away, but they didn't. Oh well. There will be other times. Maybe I can get an apartment after college. That way, I can have over anyone that I want.

It's Xmas vacation. I'm starting a new semester in less than two weeks. I'm curious to see who'll be in my classes. The FTC hasn't been together as a group since all of us were at Dade Woods. Outside of school, I haven't seen Lauren. I also haven't heard Kyle mention her much. Maybe they never got together. I wouldn't be sad if that were the case. I may still have a chance with her.

My grades are still holding up. Owen is getting his license soon, so I hope he can cart me around. Things are looking up.

Kyle kept reading.

1-13-1996

Dear Diary,

I stopped thinking about that cremation idea. It no longer bothers me. I read into it and the idea has been around for thousands of years. It was actually pretty cool how it was used to honor soldiers long ago when they died in foreign lands. I can see the symbolism in it. There's honor in it. I'd like to be thought of as an honorable guy. I'm also claustrophobic, so I can see how someone might not want to be buried. I felt that I needed to put this in my journal. E'nuff said about that for now.

Kyle now realized that Dave must have found something special in being cremated. He didn't know what, but something interested Dave about it. He then remembered that the ashes were still on the fireplace and needed to be dealt with. He decided to read the next journal entry.

1-27-1996

Dear Diary,

Lauren is in my Advanced American Literature class. Unfortunately, she sits on the other side of the room. Teresa is also in the class, and she sits near me. I've lost interest in her. Maybe I can flirt with her to try to make Lauren jealous. Let's see. Owen ditched me the other day to hang out with some new friends. He just got his license. I kind of resent that he ditched me. I'll see if he wants to do anything next week. If he ditches me again, maybe I'll keep away from him for a while. Maybe that'll send him a signal. He isn't in any of my classes, so that shouldn't be too hard to avoid him.

I'm going to get my first cellular phone next week. It's da bomb! Dad is taking me to get it, and I'll have some sort of minutes plan. I guess it'll be expensive, so I'll have to be careful using it. I haven't seen many people with such phones so maybe it'll get me some attention.

The Winter Ball was last week, and I couldn't get a date, so I didn't go. I'm not sure if Lauren went. I doubt that her mother let her. It's such a shame. I'd love to have gone with her. I need to find a girl to go to Spring Formal with. I need to figure out a way to go with Lauren. Maybe her mom will let up on that one. Her mom knows that I'm a good guy so there's a chance. Hopefully Kyle or some other guy doesn't ask to go with her before I can.

Kyle had had enough of the journal entries. They were starting to make his blood boil. Maybe he'd go back and read some more later. He'd always thought Dave was a strait-laced guy but now felt differently. Dave didn't have any honor back then when it came to Lauren and friendship. The best thing to do now was sleep on it all.

Alex Again

Kyle fell asleep quickly and was woken up just after 7 a.m. by Alex dripping water on his face from a glass. Kyle rubbed the water off with the bedsheets.

"What the fuck, Alex?"

Alex backed away from the bed with a grin. "Sorry, just messin' with ya. I woke an hour ago and I'm bored."

Kyle sat up. "Don't you have anything better to do? Didn't you think that I'd maybe want to sleep?"

Alex's grin slipped away. "Take it easy, Kyle. It was just a bit of fun."

Kyle got out of bed and went to unplug his charging cellphone. There was a new text from Owen. It had arrived at one in the morning.

OWEN: Sorry I acted so weird today. I was pissed that my bank cards didn't work. I've no idea why that happened
KYLE: It's all good. These things happen

Alex was still in the room looking expectantly at Kyle. Kyle had had enough. "Are you twelve years old, Alex? Were you really that bored?"

"I guess my childhood never left me. That's what keeps me happy."

Kyle wanted to say something else that might be good advice, but he refrained. He realized Alex craved attention, no matter what kind of attention that was. One of Kyle's college friends was like that. His name was Mitch Schmidt. Even though Kyle commuted to college, he sometimes stayed over with a friend in one of the dorms. Mitch was one of those friends, and he flunked out after two years. Despite flunking out, Mitch wasn't dumb, he just partied too hard. Last Kyle heard, he ran his own business and was very successful.

"Is Lauren up?" Kyle asked.

"No, but she slept in a tank top and jogging shorts last night. I saw her sprawled out on the bottom bunk. It was a nice view."

Kyle rolled his eyes. Alex clearly didn't have an off switch when it came to women. "Don't try the water trick on her or anyone else."

"I'm not going to try that with anyone else, although it would be fun to do it to Owen."

"Yeah, well, that'd probably piss him off more than last night, Alex."

"It's funny that you say that, "Alex said as he put the glass of water on the nightstand. "I think he's having money problems."

"What makes you think that?"

Alex crossed his arms and leaned against the wall. "As I mentioned yesterday, I thought it was weird that he had no cash in his wallet. Then, of course, his cards didn't work. So, I texted Nate Pearlman; you remember him, right?"

Nate was a guy from high school who often had betting pools going on. March Madness was his favorite, but he also loved to bet on boxing and basketballs game. He had a racket, even in high school. Kyle never got involved in such things as he didn't want the possibility of losing money.

"I remember Nate. He was smart enough in high school to run small gambling gigs."

"Yes, that's him. He now does day trading in addition to gambling. I texted him last night asking if he knew anything about Owen. He told me that Owen has had some bad business ventures. He had a good amount of real estate that went south after the crash around 2008. He lost millions. I guess he couldn't let that go. He wants to make himself still look successful. His ego gets in the way. Nate said that Owen owes a lot of people money. That includes Nate. He wanted to know if Owen was still in

Woodbrook, but I told him he'd already left. He didn't ask me anything else about Owen, so I guess he believed me."

"That's fucked up, Alex. Do you owe Nate any money?"

Alex shook his head and looked towards the floor. Kyle wasn't sure if he was telling the truth.

Alex said, "I don't have a lot of money, but I wouldn't get myself into that kind of mess. Nate isn't an evil guy, but I think he knows some people who'll break legs if they don't get their money back. I've gotten into enough trouble as it is."

"Where does Nate live nowadays?" Kyle asked.

"He lives in a few places. He told me yesterday that he was in Hawaii. He also has a house in San Diego. Don't worry; he isn't coming here for Owen. I told him that I had seen Owen in Dallas. Said that I worked for a company that had me go down there to work on some IT project. I mentioned that Owen met with me for dinner, and that's where that credit card fiasco happened."

Kyle let out a sigh. "Good, then Owen won't come back to Woodbrook in the future. After tonight, I think it would be a good idea for Owen to leave here for good."

"Yes, that's a good idea, Kyle."

Alex asked, "What were you doing in the basement? I was in the kitchen when you came back up last night."

"I was too restless to sleep. I looked in some boxes."

"Anything interesting?"

Kyle shook his head. He didn't want to tell Alex about the journals. If he did, Alex might go down there and find something he couldn't keep quiet about.

"That's what I figured," said Alex. "I might go down there and snoop around later. Maybe I'll find something interesting."

Kyle pointed to Dave's room above. "I think there would be more of interest in Dave's room. He left it in pristine condition."

Kyle hoped that Dave's room would be a good distraction instead of the basement. Kyle waited for a response from Alex, but he just stared into space.

"What're you thinking about, Alex?"

Alex smirked. "I was just thinking of checking out his closet. Who knows what fun things could be in there?"

"Just be respectful. He is owed that respect. If he has something like a diary or other personal things, leave them alone."

Alex nodded and left the room. Kyle felt like a hypocrite for asking Alex to be respectful of Dave's private possessions. Even though he'd seen something about himself in the journals, Kyle knew he shouldn't have snooped. Dave wouldn't have liked it.

Kyle went to Lauren's room and saw she was still sleeping. She was sprawled out on the bed, just like Alex had mentioned.

Kyle didn't like Alex gawking over her, so he closed her bedroom door. All that Kyle wanted now was a few more hours of sleep, so he went back to bed.

Lauren's Places

Kyle's cell alarm rang at 9 a.m.. This time, he felt refreshed. After changing his clothes, he saw that Lauren's door was open and she was no longer on her bunk. He found her sitting at the kitchen table.

"Good morning, sunshine," he said, kissing the back of her neck. She looked at him and smiled.

As he joined her at the table, he saw she had a takeout cup from Starbucks in her hand. Kyle enjoyed coffee but didn't feel like having it in the morning. The drink that he really craved right now was orange juice. A cup of that and some burnt toast was always his perfect breakfast. Adding some grape or mixed fruit jelly to the toast would be even better. Unfortunately, there was none of that in the house.

"I was wondering when you were going to wake up, Kyle. Alex was up when I sat down here about fifteen minutes ago. He waved and went outside. I can't imagine what he'd be doing outside at this time."

"Maybe a walk, I don't know. He poured some water on me earlier this morning to wake me up. It really irritated me. He's never grown up. You would think that a man in his mid-thirties would know better, right?"

Lauren took a sip of her coffee and put it on the table. "Yes, one would think."

After feeling his stomach rumble, Kyle looked at the QuikEats app on his phone to see if there were any restaurants that would deliver to the house. The local restaurant, Romeo-Bravo, was on the app, so he ordered some orange juice, two poached eggs, and some wheat toast with grape jelly on the side.

Before confirming his order, he asked, "I ordered some breakfast from Romeo-Bravo. It will arrive soon. Do you want anything? I can call them back."

Lauren shook her head. "I'm fine, thank you. I don't really feel like having anything this morning."

Kyle remembered that she'd mentioned having bulimia in high school. He wanted to ask her if her eating was okay nowadays but knew that'd probably upset her. Instead, he figured she might eat some of his food once it arrived, so he ordered extra toast.

"What do you have planned today, Lauren?"

"I think I'll go around Woodbrook and look at some of the old sight. There are a few places I haven't been to in a long time."

"Would you like me to join you?"

After taking another sip of her coffee and pausing, she said, "I think I want to be alone."

Kyle sat silently, waiting for her to say why she wanted to be alone. He tried not to stare at her but couldn't help it.

"I told you before that I was alone a lot in the later part of high school," she said.

"Yes, I remember that."

"Well, there are a couple places close to my house that I'd sometimes go to when my mother wasn't around. One of them was a block away. There was this tree I used to climb that had a wooden platform like Dave's treehouse. I'd climb up and hide on one of the branches. It was in a field. I'd only go there in the summer so I wouldn't be seen. That tree is still there. I checked on it yesterday. There's now a new house just a short distance away."

"And you want to go up that tree again?" Kyle asked.

"Yes," she replied. "I want to see if I still can. Of course, it has grown, but the wooden planks are still there. I feel this is something that I must do by myself."

"Okay, I understand. Just be careful climbing it. Those planks may not be as safe as they used to be."

She nodded. "There are also two other places. One is a gazebo by the park on Elm Street. Do you know that gazebo?"

"I do."

"I used to lay down in the center of it sometimes. I saw it the other day."

Kyle used to go to that gazebo sometimes. One time, he and Alex hid there around Christmas. Alex had kicked one of the plastic Santa Claus statues in front of someone's house, and the lightbulb inside it had made a loud popping noise and gone out. The house was about three blocks away from the gazebo, so they decided to hide there in case the police came around.

"What's the third place?" Kyle asked.

"There's a shed that was in my backyard. It's still there. Unfortunately, my parents no longer live there, so I'm not sure if I can go into it. I'm not even sure who lives there now. I carved my initials in the wood on the inside of it. I want to see if those initials are still there. I did that around 1996 or so."

"That's interesting," he said. "Hopefully, it's still there. If it is, maybe you can take a picture of it."

"That's a good idea, Kyle. I also used to sneak in there at night. I even fell asleep in there once. I felt by going in there that I was being rebellious. Kind of lame, huh?"

He didn't think it was lame. It was a small adventure for her.

"It'll be something you can keep in your heart forever, Lauren."

She smiled and looked down at the table. "I just wish you'd been in more of my memories back then. I thought about you a lot after the treehouse and the walk in the rain."

"I also wish we had met up more," Kyle said. "I've been reminded of that over the past fifteen years. It happened at random times. That feeling has never left me."

Kyle noticed that she was trying not to smile.

"I never forgot you either. I used to know someone named Kyle in college, and every time I heard someone say his name, I thought of you. I also remembered you whenever I saw a treehouse or heard about Northwestern. I even dreamed about you."

"What kind of dreams?" Kyle asked, trying not to grin.

"No, not *those* kinds of dreams. It was almost always the same. I'd see you in the school halls and would never have a chance to talk with you. It was as if you were getting further and further away from me. I must've had those dreams a dozen times over the years, each time a little different. One or two times, the dream wasn't at school but at a reunion."

Kyle remembered having dreams about Lauren. "I had a few dreams about you too. One was that I saw you at a grocery store by my house. Kind of random, I guess. In the dream, you were by the vegetables, and I tried to walk over to you, but my shoes were stuck to the floor."

"Any other dreams about me?" she asked.

"Nothing concrete. I know I had more about you, but I can't remember them. I guess I will..."

They heard the front door open and close, and Kyle lost his train of thought. Alex walked into the kitchen with a carton of Marlboro cigarettes in his hand. To Kyle, it seemed like a whole bunch of cigarettes for just one person.

"You going to smoke all those?" Kyle asked Alex.

"Nah, I just bought a bunch as they were cheap, about sixty bucks. I'll take these home with me."

"Sounds like money well spent," Kyle said sarcastically.

"Yeah, well, it is. By the way, I saw Mr. Walsh outside. He asked if you were still around."

Kyle remembered that he'd promised to see him.

"Thanks, Alex. I'll go see him in a bit."

Alex left the kitchen in a hurry. Kyle wondered if Alex would smoke all of them or sell them.

"You would think he would've thought of something better to buy," Lauren said. "After all, he doesn't have much money."

They both looked at each other in silence. Kyle knew that they were both thinking the same thing. Where had Alex got sixty dollars from? Did the money come from somewhere else? Why did Alex ask Kyle to pay for dinner if he had money?

"I guess we're thinking the same thing," Lauren said.

"I guess that we shouldn't worry about it now. I just won't shell out any more money for him."

"More money?" she asked.

Kyle shook his head. "I paid for his train ticket here and his dinner. Seeing those cigarettes really pisses me off."

"That's understandable, Kyle. I won't loan him any money if he asks."

Kyle stood up as he got a text for his food from Romeo-Bravo that it would arrive within two minutes. "I'm going to go and get my food outside. After that, I'm going to Mr. Walsh's house. What will you do?"

Lauren also stood up. "I'll go visit my teen hiding spots in a bit. I'll be back around three or later."

"Enjoy you time doing that," he remarked.

"Same to you," she said and then walked outside.

Kyle ate his breakfast of eggs and toast alone. He wished that Lauren was with him, but she needed to do her thing. He didn't want to smother her by being around all the time.

Mr. Walsh

Mr. Walsh answered the door with a Budweiser in his hand. He wore dark blue jeans and a blue flannel shirt. The shirt reminded Kyle of something he'd have worn in the nineties, except it would have been unbuttoned with a T-shirt underneath. Mr. Walsh had a smile on his face that made Kyle wonder if it was because someone was visiting him. Kyle had thought about being lonely when he got older if he was still single and how it would affect him. Maybe that's how Mr. Walsh felt.

"Good to see you again, Mr. Brighton. Come on it."

The house décor looked fresh out of the seventies. The sofa and loveseat were lime green, and the rug was bright orange. There was an old-style TV; a cube with the monitor on the left side and some dials on the right. Kyle wondered if the model even had a remote control. He doubted it.

"Have a seat," Mr. Walsh said. "I'll get you a beer."

While Mr. Walsh was in the kitchen, Kyle noticed a piano at the far end of the room. On top were a few pictures, one of which was of Mrs. Walsh. Kyle vaguely remembered her from his teens.

"Here you go," Mr. Walsh said as he handed Kyle the beer.

Kyle sat on the loveseat, and Mr. Walsh sat on the sofa.

"I see you have a few others with you at the Fremont house. It's a shame what happened to Dave."

"Yes, we're getting together in tribute to him. I may be there a few more days."

"That's nice, Kyle. I wish that I still had my childhood friends around. All of them are either dead, or we lost track of each other. I grew up in Woodbrook, and I'm the only one who's still here. So many memories of this town."

Kyle took a sip of the beer. "It's nice to see them. I've been uncovering nostalgia from my teenage years."

Mr. Walsh pointed the tip of the beer bottle at Kyle. "Those are important things. Woodbrook has given and taken so much from me. I was born in Woodbrook, a few blocks away. That was in 1937. I bought this house in 1962. My parents bought their house here in 1928."

"I can imagine you've seen so many changes, Mr. Walsh. I was born in 1980 and have seen many changes."

Mr. Walsh pursed his lips. "This town has had some dark times. Still, I wanted to stay here. I guess every town has its dark times. I just hope it doesn't go down the shitter like some other towns have in this country. Luckily, industry hasn't been then biggest employers of this place."

"What do you mean, Mr. Walsh?"

After staring into space, Mr. Walsh replied, "It was a different place when I grew up. The high school was small, everyone knew each other, and there was plenty of industry here. That industry collapsed in the seventies and eighties. All the manufacturing is gone. Now, all there seems to be is services. Everything else is made in another country or in a poorer state. It's really a shame. My father used to work at the Gluck plant that used to be near Madsen Boulevard."

"Gluck plant?" Kyle asked.

"Yes, it made seats for cars and airplanes. It was here until at least the mid-eighties. It started in the twenties or maybe even earlier. Nowadays, those seats are made somewhere else. Gluck used to provide good-paying jobs for many people who lived around here. I worked there in the sixties for a while."

"I've never heard of a company named Gluck," Kyle said. "I'm surprised I haven't."

When Mr. Walsh had finished his beer, he placed it firmly on the table next to him. "Most people your age haven't heard of it. Now, everyone commutes to Chicago or some other city where they usually work a service job. It really is a shame."

"I can imagine it's upsetting, Mr. Walsh. I remember walking around Madsen Boulevard about twenty years ago and there being some empty buildings. I can only imagine what it looks like now."

"It had its bad times about a decade ago, but recently there have been some new stores. All of them offer a service or sell something that wasn't made in Woodbrook. Gluck's plant was the last place to manufacture things here."

"Did you know the owner of Gluck's?" Kyle asked.

"I didn't, but my father did," Mr. Walsh said. "Mr. Gluck was a kind and generous man if there ever was one. He came to this county when his parents wanted to escape the pogroms in Russia in the early twentieth century. He started his business on his own, and it made a lot of money in the 1920s. He was a millionaire or close to it before the Great Crash of 1929."

"Do you mean the stock market crash?" Kyle asked.

"Yes, that's right."

Kyle had first learned about the Great Depression in high school and hoped that something like that would never happen again in the United States. Unemployment had gone up to twenty-five percent, and jobs were scarce. Many people lost all the savings they had in banks and stocks. It wasn't until the outbreak of World War Two that the Great Depression started to wane.

"What happened to Mr. Gluck's business during the Depression?"

"It ground to a halt," Mr. Walsh said. "Luckily, he had millions of dollars saved and didn't lose that money in a bank. What he did next was generous."

Kyle was intrigued by what Mr. Gluck had done with his money. He always admired people who had a generous nature.

"What did he do, Mr. Walsh?"

Mr. Walsh pointed to a picture on the wall. "Gluck helped people throughout Woodbrook. Many were bankrupt, so he shared his wealth with the Woodbrook residents. Gardens were planted, tasks were done around town on his dime, and kids were given free clothes and books he bought. This included my family. My father was out of a job, and Gluck gave him a part-time job doing public works around town. Gluck employed at least a dozen people in town to do the same job as my father. A small library was also built. It was very bad here around 1933. I wasn't born yet, but my older brother was an infant. Gluck's plant opened up again in the early 1940s. Lend-Lease made it happen."

"I remember hearing about Lend-Lease in school. It was how the United States supplied the Allied nations with materials during World War Two."

"Smart boy, you are, Kyle. Mr. Gluck was a man of honor and integrity."

Mr. Walsh's story amazed Kyle. He had never heard of such generosity. When Kyle lived in Woodbrook, he had never heard of the name Gluck before. There wasn't even a street in town with that name.

"Why have I never heard of him before?"

Mr. Walsh pointed at the same picture again. Kyle couldn't see what was in the picture from where he was sitting. "There was some bitterness when the plant left Woodbrook. It was Gluck's grandson's choice to move it down to Tennessee. Over three-hundred jobs were lost. There was a street named Gluck in Woodbrook until the mid-1980s, but now it's Dell Street. That was the name of the mayor at the time. He once worked for Gluck."

Kyle stood and walked over to the picture. It was a black-and-white photo. On closer inspection, he could see a sign that said 'Gluck Enterprises' above the entrance to a building. The era looked like the 1950s due to the style of cars in the foreground. There were a few men in suits in front of the building entrance.

"Is this building still there?" Kyle asked.

"Nah," Mr. Walsh replied. "It was vacant for most of the eighties and was knocked down in the early nineties. It's been remodeled into condos. It was on the edge of town, so maybe you never recognized the old building."

Kyle had no recollection of such a building. He did remember some condos being built at the far end of Woodbrook when he was in middle school. He remembered because there was a convenience store that his uncle often stopped at for cigarettes. He'd often let Kyle get a candy bar when they were there.

Looking at a map on his cellphone, Kyle saw a Dell Street about three miles away. He suddenly recalled that the convenience store was on the other side of Dade Woods, away from Madsen Boulevard.

"I think it's strange that I never heard of the plant. I remember a convenience store my uncle took me to near Dell Street. I forget its name."

"You're thinking of Koppell Drugs. It was probably knocked down a year or so after the Gluck plant was. Condos are there now, too."

Kyle sat back down on the loveseat. "This brings back a lot of memories of the town. I wonder what it would've been like if I'd stayed in Woodbrook."

"Speaking of which," Mr. Walsh said, "how are your parents?

"They're well. They now live in Wisconsin. I see them maybe two or three times a year. My dad will be retiring soon."

"That's good to hear. I've been alone now for a few years and find myself bored. I sometimes go to the VFW and gamble at the casino a few miles away, but besides that, there's not much to do. I get calls from my kids every once in a while, but I haven't seen them in years. They both live in other states."

The sound of being alone the way Mr. Walsh was scared Kyle. He still wasn't married and had no kids. If he never had any kids, it could be a lonely life for him in his later years. Luckily, he now had Lauren, so there was some hope.

Mr. Walsh pulled out a cigar from the end table and lit it up. Kyle hated the smell of cigars but didn't want to mention it. Unlike the smell of burning leaves or wood in the fireplace, this had an overly pungent stench. If the smell became too much, he'd pretend he had somewhere else to be.

"Did you talk to Dave much?" Kyle asked as he tried to subtly keep his hand over his mouth.

"I used to say hi to him whenever I saw him outside. He sometimes had a woman with him over there. Not sure who she was, but she drove a Jaguar. I think I last saw her about a year ago. He mentioned her name one time; I think it was Christy or Misty or something like that. I said hi to her a few times too, but she never said anything back. I guess she was just a stuffy gal."

Kyle had no idea who the Jaguar girl was.

"Dave kept to himself most of the time," Mr. Walsh continued. "I believe he inherited the house after his parents died. I knew them somewhat, but they'd never invite me to their block parties. I know I was older than them, but I saw other people from our block there."

Kyle and the five others gathered once in the treehouse at one of those block parties. Kyle hadn't lived on the block, but Dave invited him over anyway. The only one of them that had lived on the block at the time was Owen.

"I'm not sure why they didn't invite you, Mr. Walsh. I was at one of those block parties. Dave had a few kids over, and we spent some time in his treehouse."

"Ah, that big monstrosity of a treehouse. I remember that being built. I walked past the house, and Mr. Fremont saw me but looked away. I hated the way he did that."

Kyle knew Mr. Fremont hadn't been the most courteous of people. In fact, he sometimes didn't speak to Kyle when he came over. "He'd ignore me too. I never thought about it much until you mentioned it."

"Well, it doesn't matter anymore, Kyle. Those days are far behind us. There's nothing we can do to change them."

After awkwardly sitting in silence, Mr. Walsh said, "Do you currently have someone special in your life?"

Kyle couldn't help but smile. "Yes, I do have someone that I started seeing recently. I met up with her by fate. I hope it works out. As with any relationship, there'll be obstacles to overcome."

Mr. Walsh coughed cigar smoke, then pointed the cigar at Kyle. "Couples always have issues. It's normal. My wife Mary and I had them. We came from different church backgrounds, but we worked it out. Some people didn't like that she was a Catholic and I'm a Methodist. Back in those days, people were much more prejudiced about religion. In fact, some of the ministers of some churches here in Woodbrook didn't want a Catholic church built. They tried to stop it by using zoning rules in the 1930s, but the parishioners were able to build the Catholic church. My wife went there weekly, and we had her funeral there."

"That's sad that people were like that," Kyle commented.

"Some of those same ministers who didn't want the Catholic church also managed to block a synagogue that Mr. Gluck attempted to have built, even though he wasn't a practicing Jew. He never really mentioned being Jewish to people after that. I found this out when I was in my twenties and stopped going to my church after that. I still believe in God but don't need to go to that church anymore. I couldn't go to a church that discriminated against fellow religions like that. I used to give them money, too."

"I'm glad this town isn't like that anymore, Mr. Walsh. I feel that we've come a long way since then."

He coughed more on his cigar. "There are still problems, but people are more accepting. At least, I think they are. I don't know many people in Woodbrook anymore. There also doesn't seem to be as much civic duty as there once was. They stopped the Fourth of July parade a few years ago. The mayor said it cost too much. Of course, he invests in other projects I don't feel need to be. They certainly aren't as important as the parade."

"What projects?"

"He has widened some roads that didn't need it, fixed sidewalks that didn't need fixing, and had a clock tower built. The clock doesn't even work anymore. He's been mayor for the last seven years, and I don't see much relevant improvement. His last name is Bentsen. Have you heard of him, Kyle?"

Kyle shook his head, but he wasn't surprised since he'd been away for more than seven years.

"Well, maybe he'll be voted out in the next election. They just need a strong new candidate. I've got a sneaking suspicion that Tom Bentsen is crooked."

"Maybe there'll be someone new," Kyle said.

"One can hope, Kyle. This town has so much potential. In the 1960s, it was voted the best town in Illinois. It had a large public swimming pool, many different restaurants, a free bus service, and a large movie theatre. Besides the free bus, all of that's now gone or modified. Even my favorite Chinese takeout place, Woodbrook Choy Suey, is gone. Even the twenty-four-hour donut shop is gone. I loved the idea that I could go there any time."

Kyle remembered the donut shop but not the name of it.

Mr. Walsh took a drag of his cigar. The smoke was becoming unbearable for Kyle. He needed an excuse to get out of the house. After looking out the window towards Dave's house, he thought about Lauren. Even though she was still out at her hiding spots, Kyle could use her as an excuse to leave.

"I'll need to be going soon, Mr. Walsh. The girl I'm seeing is over at Dave's house right now. Her name is Lauren Stratton."

After putting out his cigar in the nearby ashtray, he said, "That's nice that you have her here. I think I saw her outside earlier. Blonde hair? If so, she's a perfect likeness to her mother."

"Yes, that's her."

"Ah, yes. I never liked her mother. To me, she was a bit off. I was strict with my children, but I heard she was at another level. How did Lauren turn out?"

Kyle couldn't help smiling. "She's great. We were never an item in our teens, but we got together a couple days ago. We both live in different states, but we'll figure it out."

"That's good to hear, young man. Make it work if it's worth it. It was for me and Mary. She cared for me a bunch and looked after the house and our children. I wouldn't change my time with her for anything. If you have that opportunity, hold onto it tight. It may only come once in your lifetime. Remember, one day, you'll be in the same position as me, and you'll be looking back on your life. I'm eighty-four years old. I've seen and done a lot in my life. Live your life well with no regrets."

Kyle stood up. "I'll be going now. It was nice to talk to you. If I'm ever in town again, I'll stop by. Thank you for all the words of wisdom. This town has an interesting past."

After showing himself out, Kyle started towards Dave's house. Suddenly, he stopped and turned around, looking at Mr. Walsh's house. It hit him how important their conversation had been. Mr. Walsh had made Kyle realize he had an opportunity that would only come once in his lifetime.

Alex's Confession

As Kyle walked onto the porch and saw Alex sprawled out on one of the Adirondack chairs again. A cigarette was burning in his hand, but his eyes were closed, and he gave a grunting snore.

"Wake up, dipshit!" Kyle said.

Alex woke up, and the cigarette fell to the porch floor. "Holy shit! You saved me from getting a burn."

"You were lucky you didn't drop that on a flammable carpet or something like that," Kyle said as he stomped on the cigarette. Now his shoe would probably smell like ash, and he hated that.

"Yeah, yeah, yeah, Kyle the Pile. You don't have to sound like my mother."

As Kyle was about to open the front door, Alex said, "I need to talk to you about something."

Kyle sat down on the other Adirondack chair, his stomach in knots. "What do you want to talk about?"

He thought it might be something about Lauren. Something bad about her past or maybe something that Kyle wouldn't want to know.

"It's about me, Pile."

The feeling in Kyle's stomach bated.

"Okay, what is it?"

Alex put his sunglasses on. "Remember we talked about Owen and his money situation? Well, it made me think about myself."

Kyle suddenly thought about Mark Grennan, Lauren's ex, and how she didn't like how he was reckless with money. Owen was the same way.

"What about yourself?" asked Kyle.

"Well, I don't think I've lived a very good life. I'm not a fake like Owen, but I'm still not a very good person. I've been like that for most of my life."

"How so?"

"I've done a lot of bad things. Maybe they're coming back to haunt me."

Kyle was silent, unsure what to say next.

"This isn't the life I wanted," Alex went on. "I thought it would get better. It hasn't. I'm in my mid-thirties, and nothing has really changed. I'm still a fuckup. You have success, and the others do to a degree. Even Owen tricks people into thinking he's successful. I can't even fake it though. I'm pathetic!"

"You can always change that, Alex," Kyle said, even though he barely believed his own words. This wasn't the first time that Kyle had heard someone talk about their life in this way. He once had a classmate in law school that was very tough on himself. That toughness stemmed from his parents.

"I don't know if I can."

Kyle knew that he had to say something encouraging. "I think you need to look internally and see what you can change."

Alex sounded tearful. "I told you earlier I screwed up my carpenter job as I didn't want to be messed over by that guy. I could've just let it go. I didn't. I wanted more money. What he did was wrong, but I could've handled it better. I don't know how to do anything else besides carpentry. I told you earlier I don't have enough money to move. I think I could learn a new trade if I had some money."

Kyle could feel it coming. Alex was going to ask for money. Kyle wanted to get straight to the point. "How much do you need?"

Alex took off his sunglasses. His eyes looked red.

"I don't know."

Kyle was losing his patience. He regretted asking about the money, but knew it had to be done.

"How much?"

"Maybe five grand. Maybe a little less."

The amount wasn't an issue. The only issue was whether Alex would waste the money and ask Kyle for more in the future. He doubted Alex would even pay it back.

"Let me think about it," Kyle said. "That's a lot of money."

"Thanks, Kyle."

A smile appeared on Alex's face. Kyle didn't like the way that it was delivered; it looked smarmy. Alex had also stopped calling him Pile, so he was obviously trying to suck up and manipulate Kyle. Deep thought would be given to that decision.

"How do I know you'll be responsible with that money? Do you even have any plans on what to do with it?"

Alex tapped his sunglasses on the arm of the chair. "I've got a few ideas. Maybe learning a new trade or something else. Money has always been a stumbling block, though."

"What about your father? Have you thought about asking him for the money?"

He stopped tapping the sunglasses. "I did ask him for five thousand once. He gave it to me, but I blew it on gambling. I asked him for more later on, and he refused."

Kyle clenched his fists with frustration. "How do I know you won't blow the money I give you?"

"Look," Alex said, "you'll just need to trust me."

That wasn't the answer Kyle wanted to hear.

"Five grand is a lot of money. I don't just throw money around like that. I have some money, but I need to live my life too. I have bills and responsibilities."

"When can you give me your final answer?"

"You'll know when you know," Kyle said flatly.

Alex sat there with his mouth open. Since there appeared to be nothing else to say, Kyle stood up and walked over to the door. As he opened it, Alex also stood up.

"I hope you give me an answer soon. I need to get on with my life. You have your sweet life, so I hope I can sort my life out one day."

Alex walked off the porch towards the street. Kyle watched him walk away and out of view in the direction of Madsen Boulevard.

"God, let my decision be the right one. If I give him money, let it make him a better person." Kyle said to himself.

Five thousand dollars was a large amount, but it wouldn't break Kyle. He'd received a decent payment over a year ago in a settlement he was part of. He'd invested that money and made decent interest. It wasn't enough to live off of for the rest of his life, but it was still a good amount to give him some leeway with his decisions. He could lend that money to Alex. Did he want to make that choice, though?

Time to Burn

The next few hours passed by quickly. Kyle watched a baseball game, and no one bothered him. He hadn't seen Alex return nor heard anything from Lauren. He looked at his phone a couple of times, but there were no missed calls or texts. It was almost four-thirty and nothing. Erica hadn't come by, so he figured she was either napping or had left the house and would be back soon.

After grabbing a beer from the refrigerator, he looked out the window and saw it was cloudy. He opened the window, and the fresh scent indicated told him it would rain soon.

"I love that smell," he said to himself.

Raindrops began falling about a minute later, progressing to a downpour. He hoped it would stop soon so they could all meet in the treehouse that evening. If the treehouse was anything like it was twenty years ago, the rain would leak from the ceiling.

Just as Kyle was about to turn away from the window, he saw Tim Oates walking by, the boy who'd been working in Dave's front yard when he'd had first arrived. Tim noticed Kyle, and despite getting drenched, he stopped to smile a wave before running for shelter.

The look on Tim's face was pure innocence. Not knowing what the world really was like was blissful. Kyle missed that feeling. He'd last had it when they were on their November rain stroll.

Kyle finished his beer as the rain stopped a few minutes later and the sun began to shine again. It reminded him of being in Florida near Fort Lauderdale with his family when he was about twelve. One time, they got caught on the beach in a downpour, and ten minutes later, it was sunny again.

By five p.m., there were still no texts or calls from Lauren. He looked around the house for her, but she wasn't there. The only person he could find was Erica. She was napping in her room, so Kyle let her be. If she wasn't up by six-thirty, he'd wake her. As for Alex, it was a wonder where he was.

Before going outside, Kyle sent a text to Lauren.

KYLE: I hope all is well. I'm at the house. Erica is napping. Alex hasn't been here for hours.

About a minute later, she responded.

LAUREN: I'm in the parking lot of a Walgreens. I stopped here because of the big downpour we just had. I've finished my exploring. I called Taylor earlier. I'm leaving here now. C ya soon.

Kyle went outside to the backyard. He was anxious to go to the treehouse but knew waiting for the other four was best.

The backyard looked mostly the same as it had all those years ago. One of the trees still had the wooden planks leading up to the treehouse. The treehouse itself was supported by three trees. They looked like hands sprouting from the ground, collectively raising the wooden structure. The small red toolshed was still there, and so was the cement bench and birdbath near the base of the treehouse. The only thing that looked different was the grass was now patchy, probably due to neglect or more shade from the surrounding trees.

A few cigarette butts lay on the ground around the base of the plank tree. Kyle remembered Alex smoking around there the day before. There was also a small empty bottle of vodka next to one of the cigarette butts. Alex's littering bothered Kyle. He picked up the butts and the bottle and put them in the green plastic garbage can that leaned against the house. As he dropped them into the can, he saw the old BMX poster that was once in the treehouse poking out of the garbage. He carefully pulled it out. Kyle had always liked that poster and felt it was a waste to throw it out. The only problem was that it was now wet, faded, and torn. Kyle dropped it back in the can.

"I saw that up in the treehouse. It was in bad shape," Alex said.

Alex's clothes were drenched, and his hair was clumped together.

"Why did you go up there, Alex?"

"I was up there yesterday having a cigarette. It looks pretty much the same except for a calendar from 1998, which was maybe a year after I'd last been up here. I didn't touch anything else except for that poster. I never really liked BMX anyways."

Kyle clenched his fists. "You should've let it be. I doubt that Dave would've wanted it thrown out. You know he liked BMX when we were in junior high."

"Well, I guess I made a stupid mistake. Let's forget it. It triggered me, that's all."

Kyle could see Alex was hurting. 'I didn't mean to make you feel bad, Alex. I guess I'm just feeling a little protective of Dave and our childhood after everything that's happened recently. What's up?"

"As I said before," Alex said. "I never liked BMX. However, when Dave got his bike when he was about ten, he'd often rub it in other kid's faces. His family always liked to show off their money. It's the same way that Owen acts; the only difference is that he doesn't have as much money as he'd like people to believe."

Kyle could sympathize with Alex about not liking how Dave bragged about his bike. Kyle never remembered Dave bragging about money, though. As for the poster, destroying it seemed bitter and petty about something that happened when they were kids. Not wanting to seem petty himself, Kyle decided to let Alex's behavior go.

"It is what it is, Alex. It can't be undone. Are you going to go inside and dry off?"

"Yes, I'll take a hot shower and put on some dry clothes. What'll you do?"

Leaning against the tree, Kyle said, "I guess I'll stay out here for a bit. Lauren will be back soon. Erica is napping, and Owen will be here around seven."

Alex stared up at the treehouse.

"We really did make a promise, and now we have to keep it," Alex said. "We were young and stupid but also had the best intentions."

Kyle nodded, and Alex walked away. The sound of the house's side door closing followed moments later.

Kyle stepped away from the tree, his right foot submerging into a boggy puddle. He immediately pulled his foot out and cursed. After the water settled, he could see his reflection in the brown murkiness. It was the same reflection he saw one day in August of 1995.

August of 1995

"Make sure you don't step in that puddle, Kyle!" Dave said.

The reflection of Kyle's face was perfectly clear in the small pool of water. It had rained earlier that day, and now it was sunny and balmy outside. Dave's parents were having a block party, and Kyle was outside with Dave, Owen, and Alex. Laughter from the adults could be heard, separate in their own little worlds from the teens. All four of the boys were bored hanging around the house, so Dave suggested they check out his new treehouse.

"So when are we going into your glorious treehouse?" Alex asked Dave, pointing up at the structure and rolling his eyes.

"Just wait a few minutes for the other two."

Kyle wondered who else would be joining them. Simon Park from across the street might be one of them. On the other hand, Simon's mother often wouldn't let him come to Dave's house, making him study instead. There was also Pat Donnelly, who lived down the street, but Kyle thought he was on vacation with his family. Pat was pretty shy, so it took a lot for him to come over. He and Dave liked playing hacky sack in the school parking lot, but Kyle found it boring.

"It's not one of your ugly girl cousins, is it?" Alex asked.

Dave flared his nostrils. "No, and don't go there, dickhead!"

"Who is it then?" Owen asked, leaning on the tree with the wooden planks.

"Just wait and see," Dave replied.

"I'm gonna go home if I need to wait any longer," Alex bluffed.

Dave said, "You can always leave now. No one is keeping you here." He gestured towards the street.

"Okay, I'll stay," Alex said as he looked down at the wet grass.

"Another thing, Alex," Dave said. "I don't want to hear any more of your mean jokes. You've got a knack for finding the worst flaws in people."

"Whatever you say, Dave. Whatever you say. I just call it as I see it. Why are you buggin' about the way I am?"

Dave shook his head and said nothing.

"Hiya, boys," a female voice said behind Kyle.

Kyle turned and saw two teenage girls. One was a girl he had never seen before. She had an olive complexion and a few pimples on her forehead. Her midriff was showing in her cropped Nirvana t-shirt and high-waisted jeans. Her smile presented her perfectly white teeth. Her jelly sandals were dirty, and her shiny hair was held up with a butterfly clip.

"I'm Erica, and this is Lauren," the olive-skinned girl said for the benefit of those who didn't know them.

Kyle already knew Lauren. She was dressed more modestly in a plain black t-shirt and tan capri pants. A light blue scrunchie was wrapped around her right wrist. Kyle thought she looked pretty because she wasn't trying too hard, unlike some girls he knew at school. Her hair was golden blonde and looked like something from a shampoo commercial. She also had braces, which he normally didn't like on a girl, but they seemed to shine on her. They'd been in a few classes together but had never talked to each other outside the classroom.

"I've seen Lauren around but never met you before, Erica," said Alex. Kyle was surprised that Alex didn't make a joke at their expense.

"I go to Sacred Heart," said Erica. "It's one town over. That's why you've never seen me."

The teens all looked at each other awkwardly. Kyle wanted to break the tension but was too worried to open his mouth in case Alex humiliated him.

"Hi again, girls," Owen said.

It's been a while, Owen. It's good to see you again," Erica said.

Dave pointed up at the treehouse. "Wanna go up there now? I doubt you two want to go into my house and see all my parent's boring friends."

"I'd love to meet your parents and their friends. Not!" Erica joked.

Dave climbed first up the planks that led to the treehouse. Owen went next, followed by Alex, Erica, and Lauren. Kyle was last, hoping there would be a spot next to Lauren. Once he got up there, he saw a space next to her, so he grabbed it. He tried not to make eye contact with Lauren as he sat on the wooden floor. Owen was sat on Kyle's left. Next to Owen were Erica and Dave. Alex was in a little nook a few feet away from everyone else.

The inside of the treehouse was empty except for a BMX poster, a portable radio with a CD player, a small wooden table, and a red spiral notebook resting on a wooden bench. There was room for at least three or four more people. The ceiling was about six feet tall, and there were two windows without glass were on the wall so that they could see into Dave's house.

"This is a cool place," Owen said.

Dave tapped his foot on the wooden floor. "Damn right, it is! My dad spent a hella lot of time building this. I helped a bit, but it was mostly him. I'd like to take credit, but I won't in this case."

"I agree, Owen. This is like some kind of clubhouse. I wish I had this as a kid," Erica said.

Kyle noticed Erica stared a lot at Owen. Alex kept his eyes on Erica.

"Do you think that we'll have some privacy up here?" Owen asked Dave.

"Why do we need privacy?" Alex asked Owen. "You want to have an orgy up here or something?"

"No, Alex. I just want to talk freely. Some of our parents are whacked."

Lauren looked over at Kyle. She smiled quickly, then peeked out of one of the open windows in the treehouse, glancing at the house. Kyle followed her gaze and saw the house's side door and a bedroom window.

"Anything interesting outside?" Erica asked.

"No, nothing. I was just seeing if anyone was looking over at us," Lauren responded. "Some of them are getting liquored up," Dave said. "I think we can speak freely in here. This is our place; the house is our parents' place."

Dave reached behind him and removed a wooden board that clearly wasn't fastened down, though it looked like the others. Dave's hand disappeared into the floor, pulling out a stack of papers.

"I know a guy that's a year older than us. I'm tight with him. He got copies of several tests that we can use this upcoming year: geometry, history, and business class. They could be useful to some of us. Once we start school again, let's see if any of these tests help." Dave held the stack of papers in the air.

"That's the reason you brought us up here?" Alex asked with a laugh.

"No, dumbass! I just wanted to show all of you. I've got a few other things stashed in this compartment."

Owen crawled over to the compartment and looked inside. "Nice! I guess we can try that stuff out when the parents aren't so close by."

"For sure, my friend."

Kyle crawled over and looked at what was inside: Two packs of cigarettes, a whiskey flask he presumed was full, three red plastic lighters, and two unwrapped cigars. Kyle had no interest in trying anything in there. His stomach started to churn in anticipation of the peer pressure he knew was coming. He didn't want to look like a wimp in front of Lauren or have Alex tease him.

"Can we try something now?" Owen asked.

Erica also looked inside. She nodded with a smile.

Dave put the board over the compartment. "I don't want to get caught by any of the adults. Maybe in a week or so."

Kyle crawled back over to where he'd been sitting.

"What was in there?" Lauren whispered in his ear.

Kyle whispered in her ear, "Cigarette, cigars, and whiskey."

Lauren bit her lower lip. "No thanks. I don't need that."

After hearing what she said, Kyle smiled and nodded, and she smiled back.

"What're the two of you talking about?" Erica asked.

Kyle turned away from Lauren and said, "We were just saying how cool it is to be up here. I've been wanting to go up here for a while now."

"Maybe all of us can make it our special place," Dave said.

"What do you mean?" Owen asked.

Dave sat back in his original spot on the floor. "Maybe we can have this as a meeting place. A club, I guess."

"That's retarded, Dave," Alex quipped.

"Take a chill pill, Alex," Erica said. "I think it's a great idea."

Alex opened his mouth but soon closed it.

"I think it's a good idea," Lauren said.

Kyle and Owen nodded.

"What kind of club will this be?" Erica asked Dave.

"Maybe just one where we hang out. Our own little group. If we want to add other people, we can."

"Wicked idea," Erica responded. "I think it would be cool."

"Who else could be added to this group?" Owen asked Dave.

Dave looked up at the ceiling in thought. "I guess anyone we all agree on. All six of us need to agree before anyone can be added. Does that sound fair?"

"I think it does," Erica said. "There's one person we can add soon."

"Who?" Alex asked.

"I think Simon Park would like to join us."

Alex laughed hysterically, rolling onto his side. Kyle knew he was overdoing it on purpose. He had witnessed Alex doing the same thing in class a few day before. Alex later explained to Kyle that he had done it to get laughs from two girls in their class. It now felt that Alex was at it again for attention. His laughter soon subsided.

"It's not that funny, Alex," Owen said.

Alex stuck his palm out at Owen. "Talk to the hand."

"Anyways," Erica said, "let's talk more about this club."

Dave smiled. "I've always wanted to be part of a secret group. I like the idea of having something that isn't adult-led and that we can control. No one except for the six of us will know about this club. Of course, that number can change if we add someone else. Simon could be one of them. The person must be a teenager and approved by all six of us. I think that sounds fair."

"We should only initiate new members here in the treehouse," Owen said.

"I second that," Erica said.

"Everyone raise your hand if you agree that any new person must be inducted in this treehouse and we've all agreed," Dave said.

Everyone raised a hand, including Alex.

"Then it's settled, except for one thing," Dave said. "I also reckon that if anyone needs to be thrown out of the group, the leader must be there to approve it. Hopefully it never comes to that."

Everyone else nodded.

'Who'll be the leader?" Alex asked.

The answer should've been obvious to Alex. After all, the club was Dave's idea, and the treehouse was his. As soon as Alex asked the question, everyone looked over at Dave. Alex shrugged, clearly feeling stupid for asking.

"Then it's settled," Erica said. "Dave will be our leader."

Dave grabbed the spiral notebook and pen. "What should we call our group?"

"How about Treehouse Group?" Alex proposed. Kyle wasn't sure if that was a serious answer or not.

"Too simple," Dave responded.

Erica raised her hand. "Maybe Order of the Treehouse?"

Dave snickered. "I like some of that idea, but to me, it sounds like we're some group that acts like we secretly run the world."

Dave started to write something in the notebook. Kyle tried to figure out a name to offer but couldn't think of anything. When he looked at Lauren, she shrugged and smiled at him.

"How about we call ourselves the Fremont Treehouse Club?" Owen proposed.

Everyone except Alex nodded and smiled. That was the best idea yet.

"I like it," Erica said, tapping Owen on the knee. "It's your treehouse, so that works. You're awesome!"

Dave continued to write something in his notebook. Once he was done, he showed everyone what he had written. It was the letters 'FTC'.

"I think there could be a better name," Alex said.

"What do you suggest?" Owen asked.

"How about Dipshits Anonymous?"

Owen giggled, but no one else did. Erica grabbed a black pen Dave had left on the floor and threw it at Alex, striking his shoulder. "Don't be a buzzkill for the rest of us."

Alex shook his head and looked away. Kyle expected him to say something snarky, but Alex kept his mouth shut.

"Do you want to be part of our club or not?" Dave asked Alex.

Alex crossed his arms and replied, "I will be. I may just be argumentative at times."

"We can always make changes to the club," Dave said. "Nothing is perfect."

Dave turned a page in his notebook and continued to write. Owen leaned over to see what it was, but Dave pulled away, holding up a hand to signify for everyone to wait.

"I'm curious to see what he's writing," Lauren whispered into Kyle's ear.

Kyle tried to hold his smile back but couldn't. He liked Lauren getting close to him. He wondered if Lauren liked him or if she was just being friendly. He hoped there would be time later that night to talk privately with her.

"Almost done," Dave said to break the silence.

Kyle whispered to Lauren, "What classes are you in this year?"

She shook her head. "I didn't get my schedule in the mail yet. Did you?"

"Yes, I did yesterday. I guess you'll get yours soon. Maybe we'll be in some of the same classes."

"Which ones are you taking, Kyle?"

"AP Chemistry, Creative Writing, Health..."

Dave was done writing, so he interrupted their conversation. "Alright, I've written down a few rules."

"Booyah!" Owen said.

"Here is as follows: Number one, all of us must decide unanimously whether a new person can enter the FTC. The same goes for voting out a member. Number two, if a member leaves, for whatever reason, all of us must get together as a tribute to signal that the member is no longer part of the club. Number three, new members must be initiated in my treehouse. Number four, what we talk about during our meetings isn't to be discussed with other people who aren't members. Number five, all official meetings take place in my treehouse. Number six, the FTC can only be dissolved with a unanimous vote."

Erica clapped her hands. "Very good. You thought of all that very fast."

"I agree with Erica," Owen said, putting his hand on Erica's shoulder. "I'm glad you're the leader."

Kyle was impressed, too.

"What do we do if some or all of us aren't living in Woodbrook anymore?" Erica asked Dave. "Like if we move for work or something."

Dave put his hand on his chin. "That's a good question. I realize some of us may go away for college, and there may be long times when we can't see each other."

"Can't we get together even if it's not all six of us?" Lauren asked.

"Yes, that's fine. The only time all six of us need to be here is if we kick out a member, add a member, or dissolve the FTC entirely. We can still meet here if at least three of us are together. Does that sound fair?"

Everyone nodded.

Erica raised her hand. "What do we do if someone dies? Sorry if that sounds morbid."

"I guess that'll be the same as if a person leaves or gets kicked out," Dave said. "We'll all need to get together to signify that the person is no longer with the group."

"You're morbid!" Alex said to Erica.

"Whatever, Alex," she said, shaking her head.

"I guess that we can make amendments to our rules if needed," Dave said.

Owen's eyes widened. "What's an amendment?"

Before Dave could answer, Kyle said, "It's a minor change to a law or rule."

"That should be unanimous, too," said Lauren.

Dave started to write in his notebook again. "Yes, I'll add that to the list of rules. Good idea, Lauren."

"I like this," Lauren said. "It makes me feel like we're part of something we can control. There's so much in my life that I'm not in control of."

"What're you not in control of?" Alex asked her.

Lauren waved off Alex with irritation and stared down at the floor. Kyle put his hand on her shoulder, but she continued to look down.

"Is there anything else we need to add?" Dave asked everyone.

Owen said, "I think the FTC should get together a few times a year. Each time, we can bullshit with each other. I think it'll be fun."

Dave pursed his lips and closed his notebook. "I've got an idea to make all of us closer in this club."

"What?" Owen asked. "It's not some weird orgy or something like that, is it?"

Erica laughed and Owen smiled. Kyle remembered that Alex had made a very similar joke earlier, but no one had laughed that time. Alex crossed his arms and shook his head.

"No, nothing like that," Dave said. "I think there needs to be something special to unite us all here in the treehouse."

"Like an orgy?" Alex said, but no one laughed this time.

Instead, everyone stared at Dave in anticipation. "I think we should each share a secret with the group. None of us can share the secret with anyone outside of the group. Any new member must also share a secret to get into the FTC. Then, we will share a new secret with them. By new, I don't mean one that's recent, just one that was not shared before."

"I think that's a good idea," Owen said. "It shows that we can trust each other if we do that. However, if anyone shares a secret with someone outside of the FTC, that person will be kicked out forever. Also, after today, we never talk about our secret again. Not even to each other."

Kyle liked the idea but was skittish about telling them a big secret. He had a few he could share and needed to pick the one that was the least damaging.

"Raise your hand if you want to be part of this secret-sharing initiation. I think it'll make us a stronger group," Dave said.

Everyone raised their hands. Alex was the last one, and when he did, he scowled.

"Who's going to start?" Dave asked.

"You should," Erica said. "It was your idea."

Everyone stared at Dave. After clearing his throat, he said, "I stole from the school store before. That may sound minor, but over the last year, I've stolen items that add up to hundreds of dollars. Pens, pencils, a pennant, a school shirt. The last time I stole was a week ago. Mike Weston works there, and he looks the other way. He sometimes steals spare change and gives it to me. I use most of it on the vending machines. Mike and I have a system where he lets me steal, and I introduce him to girls I know."

"You're not going to introduce me to him, are you?" Erica asked.

"No, you're safe."

Erica wiped her forehead jokingly. "Good, that guy is nasty."

"Didn't Paul Becker get fired from there a few weeks ago for stealing?" Lauren asked.

Dave tried not to smile. "Yes, and it was because of Mike Weston and me. I feel bad about it."

"That's shitty, but I guess it's a deep secret," Erica said.

Kyle wondered if Dave had ever stolen from him. He had been in Kyle's house before and there were many things he could have stolen, such as baseball cards and comic books. There were also a couple jars of coins that Kyle collected over the years. From what Kyle could recall, he didn't notice anything missing from his collections. There was probably no way that Kyle would ever know, though. He tried to get that thought out of his mind.

"Who's next?" Dave asked.

"I'll go next," Erica said.

"Go ahead," Dave said.

Erica shook her head. "This goes out to no one outside of here. I mean it."

"Okay, don't worry. It's in the rules. Just tell us," Dave responded.

"I have a stealing problem, too. I've stolen cash from my parents many times. I also stole from my grandmother once. None of them have ever asked me about it."

"You stole from your grandmother?" Alex asked in shock.

"Yes, Alex. We're supposed to be truthful here. I can't wait to hear what you have to say."

"Okay, I'll go next," Alex said.

"I can't wait to hear this," Erica joked.

Alex's demeanor changed. His shoulders hunched over as he looked at the floor. "What I did was something I wish I'd never done."

"What was it?" Owen asked.

Everyone's eyes were glued to Alex.

"Do you guys remember Johnny Kovacs?" Alex asked.

Everyone nodded, except for Erica.

"Well, I did something to him. It seemed funny at the time, but it was bad. I..." Alex's hands started to shake.

"You don't need to tell us if you don't want to," Lauren said.

Alex sat on his hands to stop them from shaking. "No, I'll tell you. We all promised to tell a secret."

"Please tell us," Lauren said.

"I invited Johnny to meet me and a few others at a park a few towns away. We said that all of us would be drinking and that if he was cool, he'd join us. At first, he told me that he wasn't interested. I kept asking him to go, and he eventually said he'd meet us there. Me and two other guys went to the park beforehand so we could ambush him. We brought tomatoes, rotten apples, and dogshit to throw at him. I told him to meet us at the park's canopy. Once he got there, we snuck behind him and threw all that stuff at him. One of the tomatoes knocked his glasses off, and he fell to the ground. One of the other guys grabbed Johnny's bike and rode away with it. I told Johnny to not tell his parents, or we'd ambush him again at school. We left him there to walk home. I never heard anything from him since."

"He's no longer at our school," Owen said. "I haven't seen him since the end of freshman year. Did this happen around that time?"

Alex looked at Owen then looked away. "Yes, this was right after school got out after freshman year. All I know is that he went to another school."

Erica sneered. "That was a shitty thing to do! You should find out where he is and give him his bike back. I didn't even know the guy, but I feel bad for him."

Kyle remembered Johnny. He was really short and had bottle cap glasses. He also walked with a slight limp that people would make fun of. He was in some of Kyle's advanced classes and often kept to himself, which was probably why Kyle hadn't thought about where Johnny was until now.

"That's my secret," said Alex. "No one else except the two others who ambushed him knows about it."

"Who were the other two people?" Erica asked.

"Don't go there," Alex responded. "It's no one here. I wasn't the one who took the bike, so it's probably in some landfill or something by now."

"Then you should ask your friends where it is," Erica ordered.

"Next person's turn to confess," Alex said, looking at the floor again.

Kyle still hadn't thought about what to say. He hoped one of the others would go next.

"Okay, I'll go next," Owen said.

Kyle breathed a sigh of relief.

"By accident, I saw one of our teachers around town with someone who isn't her husband. I saw them all over each other in his car. I know this guy isn't her husband because I looked at her Facebook account. The guy she was with was an older man, maybe in his fifties. I saw them leave McCallister's bar. I hid around the corner and waited for them to leave. When they did, I trailed them. They went to a motel about a block away from McCallister's. I forget the name of the motel."

"Who's this teacher?" Alex said with a bright smile.

"I knew you would ask that," Owen responded. "I can't tell you. If the details get out, it could break up a marriage, and I'd get in deep shit."

"Why are you telling us then? It isn't really about you, so the burden is on someone else," Dave said.

Owen's eyes got wider. "Because it has been very difficult to keep that in. I don't really want it to get around. This is a nice teacher."

"Is she one of your teachers now?" Alex asked.

"Drop it! That's my secret, and that's all I'll say."

"Dude, you should keep it a secret," Erica said, putting her hand on Owen's shoulder.

"I will," Owen replied, putting his hand on Erica's knee. Kyle realized they were flirting.

Dave looked at Lauren and Kyle. "The two of you haven't shared yet. Who'll go first?"

Kyle still hadn't thought of what to say. He could feel his face getting red. "Give me a minute."

He hoped Lauren would volunteer to go first, but she just stared at him. Kyle wanted to get it out of the way, but he didn't want any of his secrets to turn Lauren off. Suddenly, something came to mind.

"I have a secret that I want to share. It's from when I was younger. Some people might think I'm lying."

"What's the 4-1-1?" Erica asked.

Kyle felt embarrassed but knew it wasn't as bad as what the others had shared. "Everyone thinks that I've always done well in school. The truth is that I was a slow learner at first. It took me a bit longer than everyone else to learn to read. My mother took me to a specialist on Saturdays to catch up. Not too many people know that. Luckily, I caught up quickly. I'm embarrassed about it and never told anyone. Some people might have thought I had some learning disability or something."

"I never would've thought you had that," Dave said.

Kyle took a deep breath. He was glad that someone other than his family now knew. It was also a safe secret that Lauren wouldn't hold against him – he hoped.

"I guess you're only average in school now," Alex joked.

Kyle wanted to insult Alex back, but held it in. He knew there were plenty of things to mention, such as his poor spending habits or his lack of respect for others. Instead, he gave him the middle finger.

"Now it's your turn, Lauren," Dave stated.

Lauren hugged her knees, resting her chin on them. "I used to have social anxiety. Not your standard social anxiety, either. I'd often skip birthday parties because the thought of them would make me shake. I know it sounds crazy. What kid doesn't like birthday parties? Luckily, I was able to get over it. I started small and worked my way up to bigger events like sports games. I still get anxious a bit. I was even nervous about coming over here. Luckily, my mom talked me into going."

Kyle put his hand on her shoulder. She took her head off her knee and a tear fell down her cheek. "This group helps with my anxiety. A couple of years ago, I don't think I would've told anyone this. I never even told my parents about it."

"Your secret is safe with us," Kyle said. "As Dave said before, we're not to talk about our secrets to anyone or each other. All of us must stick to that."

"Thanks, everyone," Lauren said as she wiped away the tear.

Dave extended his hand out to the middle of the group. "Put your hand in to keep that promise and cement the oath. Once you do, the Fremont Treehouse Club will be official."

Lauren put her hand on Dave's first. Kyle put his on hers, then Owen was next, followed by Erica. The only one who didn't was Alex.

"Don't be bogus, Alex. Come over here," Erica said.

After staring into space for a second, Alex reached over and put his hand on top of Erica's. The six of them were all together now in a circle.

"As the leader of the Fremont Treehouse Club, I declare our group official. We shall promise to keep the secrets we shared today until the day we die. We also agree to meet up if one of us dies. For now, our circle is complete. If one of us dies, the circle is broken in the FTC until it's formed again with the remaining members. Remember those words."

Everyone in the group said they agreed with Dave's statement.

"So now we're an official club," Erica said. "I hope that we can meet again soon."

Everyone pulled their hands away. Dave said, "As long as at least three of us are together, it can be an official meeting. I hope to get all six of us together again, but three, four, or five will do."

"What about adding someone?" Owen asked. "I do have someone who might want to join."

Dave sat on the wooden table. "We'll all have to meet to agree on it. I'll get ahold of everyone if there's a possibility."

"Lauren?" a voice called out from the house.

Lauren looked out the treehouse window. "It's my mom. I need to leave here soon."

"Will she start buggin' out if you don't go down there?" Alex asked.

"Yes. I'll go down there in a few minutes. She'll get on my case if I don't."

"It's all good," Dave said. "I've got a taste for a beer…I mean a soda, so I can go to the house with you and get one."

Before leaving the treehouse, Lauren stuck her head out of the window. "Mom, I'll be down in a few minutes."

Dave left the treehouse first, followed by Alex, Erica, and Owen. Kyle waited for Lauren to leave, but she waited for him to go first.

"I really enjoyed this evening with everyone," Lauren said to Kyle. "The FTC is a good idea. I hope we can meet up again soon."

Kyle's heart started to beat fast. "I liked it too. I enjoyed talking to you. Shame it was only for a short time."

"Yeah, it will be nice if we're in some of the same classes this year. You're in mostly advanced classes and I'm not, though."

"Well, even if we don't happen to be in the same classes, we can always get together for the FTC," Kyle stated.

Instead of climbing down the planks, Lauren sat on the wooden floor. "Yes, we should really try that."

Kyle sat next to her. "I'll ask Dave if we can all meet after school starts. How does that sound?"

"Great," she replied. Her response was not very convincing, though. She cracked a smile for a second, but it quickly faded.

"Is everything okay, Lauren?"

"No, everything isn't okay. I don't want to talk about it right now, though. Sorry."

"Lauren, are you coming down?" her mom called from below the treehouse.

Lauren got up. "Sorry, I must go. It was nice talking to you. I'll see you around school soon."

She climbed down the treehouse planks and disappeared out of view. Kyle waited before looking out of the treehouse window. In the distance, he watched Lauren get into the passenger side of her mother's car. Their eyes met, and they waved to one another before the car pulled away.

Back in the Treehouse

As Kyle stood under the tree reminiscing, the others all arrived at the base of the treehouse. Kyle didn't notice any of them until Lauren stood next to him.

"Were you in a trance?" Lauren asked Kyle.

"I guess," he replied. "I was just thinking about the last time all of us were gathered in the treehouse."

Owen started to climb the planks. Kyle watched him go up and wondered if his weight would break any of the planks. Grimacing at Owen's every step, he finally got to the top. Kyle wondered whether Owen might get stuck in the opening, but he managed to squeeze through. Erica followed him, and Kyle motioned for Lauren to go next. She climbed up the planks easily, and Kyle followed her. Alex climbed up last.

The inside looked the same, except, or course, the BMX poster was gone, and the wooden table was no longer there. In its place was a red plastic chair with metal legs suitable for a fifth grader. Either of the two women could sit in it, but it would be too small for the three men.

"It's been too long since I was up here," Owen said. "I came up here after our first meeting but only maybe two times after that."

"I was never up here after that night," Lauren said.

"I was up here a few times," Alex said. "I was up here earlier today. Before today, I was maybe up here a half dozen times."

Kyle had only visited the treehouse two more times that he could remember. One was a meeting about a year after the first one. Only he, Dave, and Owen had been up there. They hadn't talked about much. Dave and Owen had smoked some cigarettes. The second time was just with Dave. Dave had said that he wanted to tell Kyle something, but he never mentioned what it was. Kyle had wondered about that for years. After seeing those old notes, it might have very well been about Lauren. When they were in the treehouse, they'd drunk some whiskey from a bottle Dave had smuggled from his parents. Kyle was pretty sure that it was after the dates in the notes. Dave drank so much that he passed out for a while. Had Dave not gotten drunk, he might have told Kyle whatever it was that was on his mind. Looking back, it was not one of Kyle's best times. He thought the whiskey tasted like turpentine.

"I was up here for at least one meeting," Kyle said.

"I had a few joints up here with Dave," Alex said. "That's probably why I've been up here more than any of you."

Erica giggled, covering her mouth with her hand.

"What's so funny?" Alex asked.

Erica sat on the small chair. "I've never told anyone this, but Dave and I made out up here one time. I haven't thought about it for years. It wasn't that good, so I guess I repressed that memory until now. As for other meetings, I never showed up. I wish that I had."

"It's too bad that we never all met up again," Kyle commented. "Maybe we would've added other people to the club as well."

Erica nodded her head. "I agree. Despite all of us meeting together once, it did have power. In fact, it's what brought us together here now."

"I'm amazed that we were able to pull it off," Owen said.

"How so?" Erica asked.

"Because we were all able to get here within two days. Usually, I'm not able to change my plans that fast."

"It's because our meeting all those years ago meant something," Erica said. "At least it did to me. I kept my promise and came back here."

Alex shrugged his shoulders and went over to the compartment in the floor where Dave had stashed items when they were teens. He removed the board, peeked inside, then quickly put it back and sat down.

"Nothing in there?" Owen asked.

"Nothing at all. I was hoping for some nostalgia."

Erica started to gently knock her hand on the wooden floor. "I really thought that the FTC had potential, but we never met again."

Erica was right. They had all made a big deal of the FTC, but it had never become what they'd wanted it to be. The only time that all six of them were together was that one November when they'd walked around.

"It did have potential," Owen said. "I enjoyed that night. We formed something that was only ours. No one could take that away from us."

Alex shook his head again. "To be honest, Owen, you started to move away from all of us not long after we took that long walk past Madsen Boulevard. You started hanging around other people after you got your license, like Glen Shermer or whatever his last name was. It was like you forgot about me."

"It was Glen Scherner, dickhead!" Owen responded. "Teenage friends grow apart sometimes. It happens."

"Owen is right," Erica said. "I wished that I'd stayed in touch with all of you. We can always start again, though."

"Even me?" Alex asked her.

"Yes, Alex. I forgive anything that you've done. If I've done anything bad to you, I'm sorry. The same goes for everyone here."

Lauren put her hand in Kyle's. "I've something to tell everyone here."

She quickly glanced at Kyle before saying, "Kyle and I are officially dating. I thought about keeping it a secret, but I feel that none of us should keep secrets anymore. I've liked him since I was a teen."

Erica's eyes were as wide as her smile. "Wow! Congrats!"

Kyle was surprised but also relieved. There wouldn't be any more secrets about their relationship now.

Alex shrugged and looked away. Owen bit his lip and stared at Kyle. The silence made Kyle nervous. He hoped someone would say something to break the awkward mood.

"I'm sorry we didn't tell you earlier, but it didn't feel right until now," Lauren said. "There shouldn't be any secrets between us."

"Just like how we each shared a secret in this treehouse to form the FTC," Alex pointed out.

Lauren nodded enthusiastically. "Yes! We did do that. I almost forgot. I never told anyone those secrets. I kept that promise for all these years."

"So did I," Kyle said.

"Ditto," Erica added.

Owen raised his hand into the air. "I kept the secrets, too. To be honest, I forgot what most of you said. Even if I hadn't, I wouldn't have told anymore."

Everyone looked at Alex, who was still quiet. He started to fidget, wiggling his feet. Kyle had the feeling Alex had leaked their secrets.

"What about you, Alex?" Lauren asked.

Alex cracked his knuckles. "Same as Owen, I don't even remember what secrets we told, including mine."

Kyle said, "Remember, we all agreed not to talk about our secrets again. It was only a way for us to be closer."

Alex hung his head and put his hand over his eyes. "You're right, Lauren. No more secrets. I do remember what I told you all, and I need to talk about it. It's my secret, so I feel that I can."

"Okay, go ahead and say what you need to say," Kyle said.

Alex sniffed awkwardly. "Johnny moved away shortly after we attacked him. I heard that the incident caused him a lot of trauma, and his folks decided to move to a different town. I also heard that he eventually got over it, but did you guys hear what happened to him a few years later?"

Everyone looked at each other, shaking their heads and shrugging.

"He died when he was about twenty-one. He was in a car accident while he was away at college."

"That's awful Alex," said Erica. "But Johnny's death had nothing to do with you and what you did."

Tears welled in Alex's eyes. "That's true, but I never got a chance to apologize to him. I should've. I tried to think of ways to apologize, but I never did it. The other guys with me that night told me not to apologize. I listened to them."

"Who were those other guys?" Owen asked.

Kyle held up his hand. "You don't have to tell us that."

"One last thing," Erica said.

"What is it?" Alex asked.

Erica let out a sigh. "Do you know what happened to the bike?"

Alex nodded his head. "I was given the bike a few weeks after I told you guys about what happened. Dave took it and put it in the basement here."

"You should see if it's still here," Erica said. "I think you should give it to his parents or something like that. It's the right thing to do. I'll leave that for you to decide."

Everyone was silent. Kyle remembered that the five of them hadn't fulfilled the promise that they made to Dave.

"I want to keep the promise that we all made to Dave. Now that we're all here, let's make sure that the circle is no longer broken."

Kyle stuck his arm into the middle of the group. Lauren put her hand on his, then Owen put his on top of hers. After a few seconds of wiping the tears from his eyes, Alex put his hand on Owen's, and then finally, Erica joined her hand to the pile.

Kyle took a deep breath. "The circle is no longer broken. All of us have kept our promise, and it's once again a complete circle. The FTC is still around, and we are still members."

"Amen," Erica said.

"Still complete," Owen said.

Tears spilled from Lauren's eyes. "This was a beautiful experience. Dave would've been proud."

"He would've," Alex commented.

Kyle felt compelled to say something. "We all need to promise to come together if the circle gets broken again."

Everyone agreed.

"Who's our leader now that Dave is no longer with us?" Lauren asked.

No one took any initiative, so Kyle raised his hand. "I'll do it if no one else wants to. We need to keep this going."

"Thanks, Kyle," said Erica. "We once talked about whether we should add anyone to this group. Do you think we still should?"

"Well, we're now all adults," Kyle replied. "I'm not sure if it has the same romantic idea that it had when we were teens. I guess it was a product of our youth. I don't want the group to disband, but I think it's something we can keep amongst ourselves."

Alex nodded. "Good idea. Even though I didn't realize it was important to me as a teen, I think it's special now. I even forgot the name of the club one time. I've messed up many things in my life, but this is something no one can take away from me. I'm not all jokes. I've been trying to mature, but it's difficult sometimes to change that."

"It was something that I've sometimes thought about in my adult life," said Erica. "I've never told anyone about it or what we talked about. It was our unique thing. I hold it in my heart."

Kyle was about to respond when his attention was diverted by a small metal box in the corner of the treehouse. He picked it up and saw that it was unlocked.

"What's that?" Owen asked.

"I won't know until I open it."

Everyone nodded, and Kyle slowly opened the box. Inside was a folded-up note. Kyle took it out and opened it. He read it aloud.

"Dear all,

If members of the Fremont Treehouse Club are reading this, please continue. If you're not part of that group, I respectfully ask that you put this note back in the box unread.

My cancer is getting worse, and I'm not sure how long I have left. I wanted to write this letter so that the remaining FTC members can read my last thoughts. I hope that at least one member of the FTC finds this.

From day one, the FTC was special to me. We were all together that night and made a pact. I hope that the five of you are here now reading this letter. If you are, I want to say thank you. I often think about the FTC and how it was something we shared with each other. Although the six of us were never together in the treehouse again, the FTC still lives on. The circle will be broken when I pass, but if you all get together again, it'll be complete once more. Please promise to meet again if a member passes away.

Since I was the leader, I nominate Kyle Brighton as the new lead. If he doesn't accept it, I hope someone else will take the honor. That's my dying wish.

It was unfortunate that the six of us were only together one more time. I'll cherish that rainy November day, too. It was too bad that life made us drift apart. I hope that everyone here is happy and where they want to be.

I know that the idea of the treehouse and house belonging to someone else may come up. You won't need to worry about that. I've put it in my will that one member of the FTC can take ownership. If you talk with my cousin Genevieve, she'll tell you the details. I hope that someone accepts ownership of the house. The FTC will live on!

I bid farewell. I love you all.
-David Fremont

Kyle folded up the letter and put it back in the box. He looked down, holding in the tears. He could hear Lauren sniffling.

"That was beautiful," Erica said.

"It was, and I'm honored to take the lead of the FTC," Kyle said.

"So he left the house to one of us?" Alex asked.

Kyle nodded. "It seems like it. His cousin Genevieve said that the house would be given over to someone within ten days of her calling me. That person must be one of us. It's the right thing to have this property stay with one of us. It's what Dave wanted."

Owen said, "How do we decide who gets the house?"

"I've no idea," Kyle said. "Maybe Genevieve will know. There's bound to be some sort of stipulation."

"I can tell you this," Erica said. "I've never been someone to manage property. You can count me out."

Kyle thought about whether Owen was going to fight him over the house. Since Owen was having financial issues, letting him have the house might not be a good idea. He might sell the house to get some cash. Kyle had a feeling that Dave didn't want the house to be sold. Alex also didn't seem responsible enough to own property.

"I wish that I could know now," Alex said. "I could use a place like this."

Before Kyle could comment, Erica said, "How will you deal with the property taxes and stuff like that?"

"Let's just wait until the will is read," said Kyle. "They can probably do it through a web meeting so we can all be present."

"Maybe there'll be a vote on all this," said Owen. "That's the only way it will be fair. After all, we were supposed to vote on stuff in the FTC."

Kyle noticed that Owen was inching closer to Lauren and felt his blood boil. He knew Owen wouldn't respect Lauren's boundaries despite her announcing their new relationship. Once Owen got within an inch of her, she moved closer to Kyle.

Kyle put his hand out. "We need to respect the way Dave wanted it to be for the house, no matter what the outcome. Do I have a promise from everyone?"

Lauren and Erica put their hands in. Alex added his, and after a slight pause, Owen did too. They nodded, then pulled away their hands.

"Okay, I think we're done in here," Kyle said.

"What?" Alex asked. "That's it?"

Kyle put his hand in Lauren's. "We kept our promise to Dave. The FTC is complete again and will continue to be. I'm glad we were all able to get together again. Hopefully, we'll be able to get together soon."

"If I get the house, all of you're welcome here anytime," said Owen. "I must leave tomorrow, so let's see what happens with the will next week." He got up and climbed down the planks. Alex followed, then Erica, leaving Kyle and Lauren alone in the treehouse.

"This is just like it was back in 1995, Kyle. We were the last two to leave the treehouse. My mom called for me, so I had to leave. I really wanted to stay up here with you that night."

"I felt the same way, Lauren. After that night, I only had one really good conversation with you when we went on that walk. I got to know you a bit better that day, but it wasn't enough.

I should've made an effort. I saw you around school, but I didn't do much more than say hi."

Lauren leaned over and kissed him on the lips. "Well, we have the present. Can I stay with you in your room tonight?"

His heart jumped. "Of course. I want you to. I can hold you for the whole night."

They kissed again.

"I need to be honest, but I'll be glad when Owen leaves," Lauren proclaimed. "I told everyone that we were together partly because I thought it would drive him away, but he just kept inching towards me. He's so creepy."

"Yes, I noticed that. I wanted to push him away. I'm glad you moved over to me instead."

Lauren stood up. "I want you to know that I think you should get this house. I feel that you're the only one responsible enough for it."

"What about you, Lauren?"

"I need to go back to my son."

Kyle put both his hands in hers. "If I get it, I'd like for you to join me. Of course, I would also want Taylor to come, too. What do you think of that?"

"I like that idea a lot, but perhaps we should get to know each other better first. Maybe give it a few months. Taylor also needs to get to know you."

"That's a perfect idea. Let's see what happens. Even if I don't get this place, we should get to know each other and maybe get another place."

Kyle climbed down the planks, and Lauren followed. They both went back into the house, holding hands.

Departure

Kyle and Lauren slipped into bed together. They hadn't seen any of the others when they'd come inside. For the whole night, they slept soundly in each other's arms, waking gently to the sound of birds singing.

"That was a perfect night, Kyle."

While she was in the shower, he got up and went to the kitchen. There was a note on the table. The bottle of Dom Perignon was beside it.

Hi all,

I was able to move my flight to 8:30 this morning. I know I'd planned to stay a little later, but I need to get back and straighten some stuff out. I've got some old debts to deal with. I've been living a life that's way beyond my means. That isn't going to happen anymore. I'm glad we all met up. I know that all of you would've met up if I'd died instead of Dave. I'll talk to all of you in a week when we deal with Dave's will.
P.S. Someone can drink the Dom Perignon. I don't want it anymore.

-Owen

It sounded like Owen was trying to change his ways with his finances. Kyle liked that idea but would believe it when he saw it. Even if Owen did change, Kyle would still prefer not to hang around him anymore. The only reason they'd have to reunite would be if the circle was broken again.

After sitting at the table, Erica came in. She was wearing a pink bathrobe.

"You've read Owen's note. I saw him leave. He asked if he could see me if he was ever in the area."

'What did you say?"

"I said I'd think about it. He probably would've kept pestering me if I'd said no. Yesterday, I told him that I used to have a crush on him in high school. I wish I hadn't said that. He acts like my feelings have carried over to today."

Kyle laughed. "Well, I guess that was the best thing to do. It sounds like you don't want to be around him. I don't blame you."

"What's with the Dom Perignon?" Erica asked.

"Owen left it. Do you want it?"

Erica shook her head. Kyle put it in one of the cabinets. He'd figure out what to do with it later. He didn't want to give it to Alex. The guy clearly couldn't handle alcohol.

Erica fixed herself some coffee. Kyle declined a cup. "I can only take so much of Owen," Erica continued. "He tries too hard to be something he isn't. I see in his note that he wants to change, but I don't entirely believe that."

"I feel the same way."

"Besides," Erica said, smirking. "I spent last night with Alex. Owen doesn't know that."

Kyle went to the fridge and poured himself a glass of orange juice. "It was a good idea that you didn't tell Owen. Do you have a thing for Alex now, or was that just a one-time thing?"

"I think I'll be spending more time with him. He doesn't really have a steady place, so he may move with me to Orlando. We're going to talk about that later today."

After looking around the kitchen, Kyle asked, "Where's he now?"

Erica motioned her head towards the porch. "He went for a walk. He likes to do that. He's been on several since I got here."

"Yes, I've noticed."

Kyle wanted to say more but knew Erica might tell Alex. It wouldn't be long before Alex pissed off Erica. They wouldn't be a couple for long.

"What's going on with you and Lauren?"

Kyle finished his orange juice. "Her and I are going to get to know each other more. If I get this house, I'm going to move here. I'm hoping that she and Taylor can move close to here. It all depends on how things go between the two of us."

"What about your attorney job in Ohio?"

"I can quit that. I was part of a lawsuit settlement that made me enough money to keep me going until I settle on what I want to do next. I can always take the bar exam for this state and start up around here. There's always a need for lawyers in the US."

Erica laughed. "Why didn't you ask me out instead?"

"Very funny," Kyle responded.

"In all seriousness, Kyle, I think it's great. It's horrible that Dave died, but at least something good came out of it. You have Lauren, and I'll see what happens with Alex. I know he needs to work on himself, but I do, too. The tension between he and I is due to attraction. At least, I think it is."

Erica's phone buzzed. She looked at it then put it back down. "Alex wants me to meet him at a park near here. He said you would know where it is."

Kyle pointed in the direction of the park. "It's over there. Why does he want you to meet him there?"

She stood up and shrugged her shoulders. "Maybe he wants some privacy."

"Okay, have fun."

While Erica was on her way out the door, he remembered the conversation with her about Lauren's inability to have any more children. Kyle didn't mind, but he wanted to bring it up at an opportune time so as not to upset her.

The sound of the shower stopped, so Kyle waited for Lauren. She came downstairs in a white tank top and blue jean shorts.

"Hey babe, are we alone in the house?" Lauren asked.

"Yes, Owen left on an early flight. Alex and Erica are at the park."

Lauren rolled her eyes. "Yeah, Owen texted me early this morning. That guy never lets up. Check out his texts to me."

She gave her phone to Kyle.

OWEN: Hey, I'm leaving today. Sorry I didn't say goodbye. I feel that there's a connection between us. Do you feel the same?

He'd sent it at 5:23 a.m. Lauren had replied at 8:17 a.m.

LAUREN: I don't feel the same. I'm with Kyle now. We can be friends and nothing more. Sorry.

OWEN: Are you lying to me? You've got no feeling whatsoever?
LAUREN: Sorry, no.
OWEN: I can give you what you need financially
LAUREN: I'm good with money
OWEN: Whatever you say
LAUREN: Talk to you again sometime. I'm happy with what I have now
OWEN: OK, fine

    Kyle liked the way Lauren had handled the conversation. He passed the phone back, smiling.

    "You're right; he doesn't let up. It's good he's gone. He left a note this morning saying he wanted to be more financially responsible, but I doubt he'll change."

    "Yeah, he's all over the place," she replied. "I also don't like the idea that someone might be after him due to his debts. Probably the same debts that Alex mentioned yesterday. Alex mentioned someone named Nate told him about it."

    Kyle had forgotten about that. "That's also a good point. Even if he got Dave's house and didn't sell it, it might go to the debt collectors as collateral."

    "On another note," she said. "If you end up getting the house, will you move into it?" "I've thought about it, and I'd like it if you and Taylor came to visit me. I know that you and I must get to know each other better first, though. The same goes with Taylor."

Kyle knew that if things did get serious with Lauren and she moved to a new state, something would need to be worked out with her ex for parental visits. It was something on his mind, but he didn't want to bring it up just yet.

"And what about the possibility of having more children, Kyle?"

This was the perfect opportunity. Kyle didn't want to tell her he knew about her issue, so he planned to play it safe.

"Do you need to have children?" she asked again.

Kyle put his hand on hers. "I'm okay with what's good for you. If we decide that we're good for each other and stay together, then being with just you and Taylor would be perfect for me."

Lauren smiled as her eyes started to water. "You said that perfectly." She took a deep breath.

"It's how I feel, Lauren."

"About a year or so ago I discovered that I had some cysts on my ovaries. I had to have them removed. I can no longer have children. Does that bother you? I know I should've told you earlier, but I didn't want to ruin things. You told me that you wanted children. That's why I've been up and down the past few days."

The weight of the subject was now off both of their shoulders.

"I completely understand, Lauren. I want to spend time with you and for us to continue to share these moments. I must say that the last two days have been the best of my life. I'd almost given up on love. You and I meeting up again all stems back to the FTC. If all of us hadn't made that promise that one night, we never would've met up again. I know that I never would've come back to Woodbrook."

"You're right. I'm glad we met up in the park that night. To be honest, I felt something was pulling me to get here earlier. It was divine intervention, I guess. If I'd arrived here the next day, who knows how things would've played out, right?"

Kyle stood up and gently pulled Lauren to the basement. Once down there, he had her sit on the floor while he put a CD in the player. After the song started, he sat behind her and wrapped his hands around her.

"*November Rain* again, huh? I love it!" she said.

"This is our song. Next to the last few days, that was the fondest memory of my life," Kyle said.

"Same goes for me, Kyle. That and the FTC led to where we are today. I wouldn't change that for anything in the world."

Kyle had put the song on repeat. It played three more times until they heard the front door closing. Hopefully it was Alex and Erica. After stopping the song, Kyle and Lauren hurried upstairs.

A Surprising Connection

Alex was by the kitchen table, but there was no sign of Erica.

"Where's Erica?" Lauren asked.

Alex scrunched his nose. "Me and her just had a talk. She said that she needed some time alone."

"Care to talk about it?" Lauren asked.

He grabbed a beer from the fridge and said, "Both of you probably know that me and Erica are together now or are at least trying to be."

Kyle nodded.

"Erica texted me saying you guys got together last night," said Lauren.

"I know that Owen told some of you that I had a kid I wasn't paying support for. That's true. I've been a deadbeat dad, and I haven't seen my son in a long time. I gave up custody. I feel that he's better off without me. His mom is now married to someone else, so she's fine financially now. Erica asked if it was true, and I told her the truth."

"What does she want from you?" Kyle asked.

"That if me and her get serious, I won't walk out on any family we might have."

"That's up to you," Kyle said. "I'm not going to lecture you."

Alex finished his beer, put it on the table, and went over to the sink. He looked out the window, his shoulders slumped.

"Will you be leaving today?" Kyle asked to change the subject.

Alex turned around. "If she wants to leave today, I will. If she wants to leave without me, I'll stay here as long as I can. I don't have anywhere else to go."

Kyle felt sorry for Alex. He was about to say something comforting, but Alex's phone buzzed. He looked at his phone, then put it back in his pocket.

"Erica just texted me. She wants to meet outside again. I wonder what she'll lecture me about now."

"Go to her," Lauren said. "Do your best to make it work. You're the only one who can change you."

Alex left with his shoulders still slumped. Kyle and Lauren went to the living room. They spotted Erica talking with Alex through the window. The two of them joined hands and walked to Erica's car.

"I worry about the two of them," said Lauren. "I don't think that he'll ever be responsible. I hate to be negative, but that's how I feel."

Kyle put his arms around Lauren. "I feel the same way. I want to believe that he'll change. I don't want to speak bad about him, though."

Lauren kissed Kyle and said, "It's kind of sad that Owen and Alex have turned out the way they have. I do feel there's some hope for Alex, though. When we were in the treehouse and on that walk, it seemed like we'd all be friends forever. I'll always try to remember Alex, Owen, Dave, and Erica the way they were."

"I'll try to do the same, Lauren. As adults, we all seem so different. The person from the FTC who means the most to me is you. I won't forget the FTC, though. As promised, we'll have to get back together if one of us passes away. I won't break that promise."

"I'll have to leave tonight. Can we meet again after the reading of the will? I assume that it'll be done virtually."

Kyle thought about the importance of changing his life. He now had an opportunity to start a new life.

"Yes, I will see if I can resign from my firm soon. If I'm able to get this house, I'm going to move in. You can then visit me here if you'd like. If I don't get this place, maybe I can visit you in Tennessee."

"That sounds like a plan, Kyle."

The slamming of a car door made Lauren jump. They walked over to the porch door and saw Erica and Alex holding hands again.

"They must've solved their issues quickly," Kyle quipped.

"I think we should be more positive about them. I'll try to be, at least."

About a minute later, Alex and Erica walked in. Kyle didn't see where Erica went but he saw Alex go into the TV room and sprawl out on the couch soon.

"Where's Erica?" Lauren asked.

Alex pointed towards the ceiling. "She's upstairs getting her things together."

"Did she even sleep upstairs last night?" Kyle inquired.

Alex sat up and smirked. "Yes, she was with me. I thought that the two of you knew that already."

Both Kyle and Lauren looked at each other and didn't say anything.

"Well, we did. You don't have to answer me on whether you did know or not. I'm not hiding anything. I want to be an open book so no more secrets. Owen saw us last night going into the room. He gave us a hard look. That guy is so jealous. I'm leaving with Erica."

"I'm glad to hear it about the two of you," said Lauren. "It can be a new start for both of you. As for Owen, just let it be. It sounds like he has some things to sort out."

Kyle wanted to believe that it would work between them. Like Lauren had said, it was best to be positive. Kyle avoided Alex's gaze, glancing over at the fireplace, spotting the urn. He walked over to it. Since he'd read Dave's journal entry about cremation, he'd thought about what needed to be done.

The others watched Kyle as he picked up the urn. "I wonder what Dave wants us to do with his ashes."

"You don't know what to do with those ashes?" Alex asked.

Kyle's eyes widened. "No, I don't. Do you?"

Alex joined Kyle at the fireplace. "I do. At least, I remember something Dave told me a long time ago about being cremated. I'll never forget him telling me that was his wish. I didn't really take it seriously when we were teens. He said something very specific about where he wanted them to be placed."

The idea that Alex knew what to do surprised Kyle. Dave's cousin Genevieve had mentioned that Dave's friends would know what to do with them. He definitely wanted to hear what Alex had to say.

"Please tell us."

"Follow me," said Alex. He led them outside to the treehouse.

It was a perfect, sunny day outside. It reminded Kyle of how life often felt sunnier when he was a kid. Even though there were some dark days in his youth, the good days outweighed the bad ones.

"He wants them to be put in the treehouse?" Kyle asked.

"No, he wants the ashes to be scattered at the base of the tree. He told me this one time when we were teenagers. This was months or maybe a year after we started the FTC. It's kind of funny that I remember such a random thing. I'm not usually like that."

Kyle examined the base of the tree. "Why didn't you tell us this earlier? We were up there, and you said nothing."

Alex shrugged as they started back to the house. "I didn't think of it. It might be the drugs, I don't know. I need to stop those things. When Dave mentioned it years ago, I just listened to him and didn't think anything of it, but it did catch me off guard. I don't know why he said it. Out of sight, out of mind for me with such things."

Kyle didn't know the exact reason why Dave wanted to be cremated, but he remembered the part about ancient soldiers doing it to be honored in foreign lands. Kyle understood why Dave would want to feel honored.

When they got inside, Kyle sat on one of the couches in the living room and sighed.

"Are you okay?" Alex asked.

"I'm okay. I'm just glad this conversation came up. We needed to figure out what to do with the ashes. It was as if it was destiny for you to remember that conversation with Dave."

"All of this was destiny," Alex said to Kyle. "You and Lauren got to meet up, and so did me and Erica. That never would've happened if it wasn't for Dave's passing. Everything happens for a reason. We must make good out of the bad that happens to us. That may sound morbid, but it's the truth."

"He's right, Kyle," Lauren said.

Kyle knew it.

"The FTC started this," Alex said. "We all happened to meet that night, and it brought us together. Without that meeting and the November walk, these past few days wouldn't have occurred."

Kyle wondered if maybe something had changed in Alex for the better.

"The only one who didn't benefit from this was Owen," Lauren said. "I hope he turns his life around."

"Me too," Alex said. "I need to do the same myself. Maybe Erica can steer me in the right direction."

"That's good to hear," Kyle said. He hoped Erica would do just that.

After giving Lauren a hug and shaking Kyle's hand, Alex said, "I need to pack up my belongings too. We'll be leaving later today. Thanks to both of you for dealing with me now and as a teenager. I've been trying to change for years now. Erica might be the catalyst I need. I promised her that I'll get a job. I'll start looking tomorrow."

"Live your best life, Alex," Lauren said, and they smiled at each other before Alex left to pack his things.

"Maybe this will be a new beginning for him," Kyle commented. "I'll try to believe it'll work for them."

"He deserves another chance. You and I got one, so why not him and Erica?"

They hugged each other and sat on the loveseat. Lauren looked at the time on her cellphone. "I need to book a flight, Kyle. I've seen there's one at 7:30 tonight. There's also one at 5:10. Will you be able to follow me to return my car and then drive me to my gate?"

"Yes, anything for you."

"Thank you," she responded. "I hope that you can drop me off at my gate. That way, you can see me off."

Soon, Erica and Alex came downstairs with their belongings. Kyle would truly miss the two of them. Kyle was about to say goodbye but then looked over at the ashes on the fireplace.

"Before we go, I think we should do something with the ashes."

"Do you think we should scatter the ashes now or wait?" Alex asked.

Erica looked over at the mantle. "Wait for what?"

"Dave told me years ago that he would like to have his ashes scattered under the treehouse if he was ever cremated," Alex responded. "We're all here, so maybe we can do that for him."

Lauren looked dubious. "To be honest, I'm not sure. I don't know if Dave ever said who should scatter them. Maybe it should be the person that gets this house. What do you think?"

Alex walked over to the mantle. "I think that's a good idea."

"Then it's settled," Kyle said. "Let the person who gets this house do it."

They all nodded.

After everyone hugged, Alex and Erica left the house. Kyle and Lauren watched as Alex and Erica drove away.

"Do you find it weird that Alex remembered about the ashes all of a sudden?" Lauren asked Kyle.

"I don't know, it could've happened."

Kyle had wanted closure to the ashes, and that's what he'd been given. It did make sense to him as the treehouse meant so much to Dave. If he inherited the house, he would scatter the ashes at the proper time.

Kyle and Lauren were alone again. It was the perfect ending to what had turned out to be an inciteful and wonderful few days.

Just the Two of Them

As Kyle sat on the couch with Lauren, he looked over at the urn, still on the mantelpiece. Now that they knew what to do with the ashes, he thought about how one member of the FTC would disperse them.

"Lauren, I'll never forget these past couple of days with you and the others."

I feel the same Kyle. It goes to show that all of this was meant to be. I reunited with you, and Alex did with Erica."

Lauren looked at her phone and stood. Kyle knew it was getting close to the time she needed to leave. "I hate to say it, but we must leave soon."

"Which flight did you pick?"

"The 5:12 flight. That way, I can be home before Taylor goes to bed."

"Are you going to get ready now?" he asked.

"I've one more thing to do. I need to do it alone. I'll tell you about it another time. It's not even noon yet, so we still have some time to spare."

"How long will you be gone?"

"Probably one or two hours. Will you be staying here overnight?"

Kyle wasn't sure. Staying until the will was read was an option, but that might be boring if no one else was around. Staying one or two more nights seemed like a good idea as he could reflect on the possibility of getting the house.

"I think I'll stay at least one more day, maybe two. I may need some time to go home and work out the scenario of either coming here or staying in Cincinnati."

"Understandable, Kyle. I'm so excited that you have this new opportunity to potentially live here. I have a feeling that it will be you that's chosen."

She kissed him and then left the room. A few minutes later, she brought her luggage down and placed it by the door before returning to the living room.

"I'll be back soon. You'll understand later, Kyle. I'm excited about it."

He wondered what it could be. He had faith that it was something good.

"Okay, I'll be waiting for you."

"I'll be thinking about you." She conveyed a bright smile that squeezed his heart.

"I'll definitely be thinking about you," Kyle responded.

Before she left, Kyle thought about how, years ago, Dave hadn't told him that she liked him. If that had happened, that might've changed the present situation that they were in now. Maybe things wouldn't have worked out between him and Lauren in their teens. Perhaps their reunion would have been awkward and tense. In retrospect, Dave not saying anything might've been the best thing he could've done for them.

Kyle watched Lauren leave in her car. Since her luggage was still there, he knew that she'd be coming back. In his heart, he knew that she could be trusted. It was the first time in a long time that he'd had that feeling.

Leaving

Lauren returned just before 2 p.m. Kyle had watched baseball on TV, so the time had passed quickly. As soon as he heard her car door close, he went out to the porch to greet her.

"Everything okay now?"

She smiled. "Yes, I feel much better now."

The longing to ask her what she'd done burned inside him. He knew not to ask, though. "As long as you're happy."

"I am. I'll get my bags so we can head to the airport."

He helped Lauren load her trunk. Just before Kyle got into his car to follow her, he took another glance at Dave's house. He imagined sitting on the porch with Lauren, beers in hand, listening to Taylor playing with friends in the treehouse. Kyle wanted that with all his heart.

They finally arrived at the airport car rental. He waited in his car while Lauren went to the kiosk to give back the keys. Lauren smiled, talking to the attendants, and making them smile. Kyle knew his days with Lauren would be sunny.

She opened the passenger door of Kyle's car and got in. "Thank you for waiting for me. It feels so good to have someone who cares enough to help me out."

"No problem, Lauren. I'm always here for you."

They left the car rental and headed for the airport. There was a long line going to departures. Her flight didn't leave for another two hours, but there was the slight chance of missing her flight. The TSA lines might be long, so she didn't want to take a chance.

"Things might get hectic," Kyle said.

She nodded. "I don't mind at all. These past few days have been amazing. My mind is in a totally different headspace than before I got your call about Dave's passing. I'm in a much better place now."

"Me too, Lauren. I've always been missing something, and it was you. I don't think many people get to have their lives turned around in such a short amount of time. With some luck, Erica and Alex might, too."

"Yes, I hope they can work it out. Alex isn't a bad guy. He's just made some bad choices. We all have at times, though."

Kyle nodded. "On another note, I've been thinking about Dave's house."

"What about it, Kyle?"

"If I do get it in the will, I'm going to move here as soon as I can. I would like it if you visited me from time to time."

"I definitely will, Kyle. We can get to know each other more."

Kyle didn't want to be too forward. "I'm also looking for someone to start a family with."

Lauren looked crestfallen. "You know I can't have any more kids."

Kyle placed his hand on her thigh. " I know that. I meant that we could possibly adopt. That's if you're up for it?"

She smiled. "Oh my, I never thought of that. That's a great idea!"

Kyle had thought of adopting before but wanted to be married first. If his relationship with Lauren worked out, it was something he wanted to do.

"The house is big. I think it's great for kids, especially ones who've had a difficult start."

Lauren gently clapped her hands. "I've always wanted to help those who are less fortunate."

"I'm sorry if I'm being a bit forward, Lauren. I know that we just got to know each other again recently. I've never had this feeling before. It's something new to me. Please forgive me if I'm moving too quickly."

"It's ok. I want to see what'll happen."

The line to the departures started to move faster, so Kyle paid attention to the road ahead.

"Which gate are you at?"

"I'm at E9. United Airlines."

Kyle knew it would only take a few more minutes to get to the gate. He wished there was more time.

"I'll miss you. You'll be on my mind. I'm very anxious to see the result of the will."

"Me too, Kyle. Even if you don't get the house, I know things will turn out well for you. We'll also have time to get to know each other. It may take a while, but it will be worth it."

There was an opening at the United Airlines gate, so Kyle pulled over.

"I'll be thinking of you the whole time. Please text me when you get on the plane."

They both got out of the car, and he took her luggage out of the trunk.

Lauren smiled and took Kyle's hands.

"I think everything will work out with our living situation. Trust me."

"You have a way about you, Kyle. I love you."

"I love you, too."

They embraced one more time, then Lauren grabbed her luggage. Just as she was about to enter the terminal, she turned around and blew him a kiss. He did the same in return. A car honked behind Kyle's. It made him jump, and he waved to signal that he was leaving. He quickly looked back, but Lauren had gone.

After pulling out of the gate and towards the exit, he heard his phone buzz with a text. He drove to a gas station nearby and checked his phone.

LAUREN: Things will turn out all right. I've put something in motion. I'll tell you about it next week.
KYLE: I can't wait to hear about it
LAUREN: I can't wait to tell you. Love you
KYLE: I love you too

The trip back to Dave's house was quick. He remembered putting the Dom Perignon away in the cabinet, so he took it out. A second away from opening it, he suddenly stopped. It could be saved for a big occasion. He just wasn't sure what it would be yet.

He put away the Dom Perignon and looked around the kitchen. The house seemed cozy. He could see himself living there. It would be even better if he had someone to share it with.

When Lauren landed back home, she sent him a text, which made him glad she was safe. There was a void inside of him, though. He knew it would be no more than a week until he would see her again, but it felt like an eternity.

After a few hours of nothing to do in the house, Kyle decided to leave the next day. The will would be read in less than a week.

Epilogue

Kyle stayed at Dave's house for one more night and left the next day. Lauren and Kyle spoke on the phone the night he got back home. She revealed her big secret; she'd been secretly looking at houses in their old neighborhood on their last day together before she went to the airport. A realtor had shown her three different houses, all of which she might move to in the near future. She'd grown so in love with the area. She mentioned that despite having a difficult youth, she still loved and cherished the memories it gave her. The feelings of nostalgia from the area and talking to Kyle had made her feel so happy. Even if Kyle didn't get Dave's old house, he would try to move in the area that was near Lauren.

A few days later, the will was read to Kyle, Lauren, Owen, Alex, and Erica via Skype. Genevieve was also on the call. It stipulated that through a vote between them, one of the five of them would get the house. They couldn't vote for themselves. The result was four votes for Kyle and one for Erica. Owen had voted for Erica, and Kyle believed it was because he was still trying to get in her pants. All the votes were emailed directly to the lawyer reading the will. The group also found out that if the letter that

Dave wrote in the treehouse had not been found, then the lawyer would've contacted them all himself.

On the Skype meeting, Kyle watched Owen's reaction to the tally of the votes. He closed his eyes, thumped the desk, and left the meeting without saying goodbye.

Once it was official, Kyle resigned from his law firm. With his savings, he was able to move to his new house within a few weeks. He planned to take the bar exam in case he needed to go fall back on work. He also looked for a storefront to start his own sports memorabilia business. It wouldn't make him rich, but it would be some extra income.

Kyle moved into Dave's old house within a week. Lauren also moved to Woodbrook two months later. Her two-bed house was about a block away from Dade Woods. Lauren and her ex-husband worked out that Taylor could visit him during school vacations.

After taking a month off, Kyle took the Illinois bar exam and passed. He purchased a small office only four miles away from his new house. He planned to do a few cases a year, some of them pro bono.

After six months of dating, Lauren and Taylor moved in with Kyle. Three months after that, Kyle proposed to her, and she accepted. The two of them celebrated on the front porch by drinking the Dom Perignon. They were married six months later in a civil ceremony. There were only ten guests. Erica and Alex attended, but Owen didn't. No response was ever given by Owen. Kyle suspected it was probably because he still liked Lauren. Owen didn't attempt to reach out to any of them after the wedding invite. They left him several voicemails, but he never responded.

Tim Oates showed up every once in a while. He mowed the lawn and would do yard work. Kyle found out that Tim was indeed the son of Matt Oates. Matt had divorced Tim's mother and moved away to Oregon. Tim hadn't talked to his father in several years.

Alex and Erica stayed together. He got his real estate license and made a good living from it. She changed careers, too, and worked in sales for an office equipment company. They got married two months after Kyle and Lauren did, and less than a year later, Erica gave birth to a baby boy. They named him David. Alex also paid all the past-due child support he owed his ex. Kyle never lent him money and was glad he didn't have to. Alex had achieved all he'd wanted without Kyle's help.

Over three years since they'd all seen each other, Erica received a call from one of Owen's friends, Paul Andersen. He told her that Owen had been found dead in an alley in Dallas, Texas. Foul play was suspected. Paul said that Owen still owed people a lot of money. Their childhood friend was now gone. They all agreed to meet up again in Dave's treehouse. The circle was broken again.

Made in the USA
Columbia, SC
08 December 2023